Young Nick
AND
Jubilee

Also by LEON GARFIELD:

Young Nick
AND
Jubilee

LEON GARFIELD

Illustrated by

TED LEWIN

Delacorte Press

Published by Delacorte Press
Bantam Doubleday Dell Publishing Group, Inc.
666 Fifth Avenue
New York, New York 10103

Text copyright © 1989 by Leon Garfield
Illustrations copyright © 1989 by Ted Lewin

Library of Congress Cataloging in Publication Data
Garfield, Leon.
Young Nick and Jubilee / Leon Garfield;
illustrated by Ted Lewin.
p.   cm.
Summary: An opportune meeting with a pickpocket and a pupil
from a charity school sets events in motion
that drastically and irrevocably change the lives
of an orphaned brother and sister existing
by their wits in the streets of London.
ISBN 0-385-29777-7
[1. Orphans—Fiction.   2. Brothers and sisters—Fiction.
3. Robbers and outlaws—Fiction.   4. London (England)—Fiction.]
I. Title.   PZ7.G17943Yo   1989   [Fic]—dc19
89-1604   CIP   AC

Book design by Andrew Roberts

Manufactured in the United States of America
September 1989
10   9   8   7   6   5   4   3   2   1
BG

TO
Rebecca AND *Gerry*

Chapter One

THEY WERE BROTHER AND SISTER; that much was for sure. They were written down in a book somewhere in Ireland—at the bottom of a bog, for all anybody cared. Laid end to end, they were about nine feet long, but separately, and standing upright, they weren't much above doorknob height.

Not that they had much to do with doors and doorknobs, as they were living rough, inside a rustling cave of ivy and hawthorn, which they shared with spiders, wood lice, and papery butterflies, on the wild side of St. James's Park in London Town.

Times were good: they were warm and dry. It was summer and late on a Saturday night. Lamps, like burning fruit, still glimmered among the shadowy trees, and flowery walkers still strolled along the paths. But not on the wild side, where all was dark and secret, as if thieves had stolen the moon.

He (that's the brother) was called Young Nick, to

tell him apart from Old Nick, who is the Devil; and she (that's his sister) was called Jubilee, on account of the Pope having done something wonderful in the year she was born. They were a bony, ragged, runaway pair, with bottle-green eyes and foxy looks, such as would have made chickens run for their lives. Folk said they were worse than animals, but it depended on your point of view.

Young Nick, who'd thieved and scrambled his way up to ten, was the older by a year, and took advantage by swearing he could remember their mother and father back in Ireland—which Jubilee knew was a dirty lie, and kept telling him so.

"I do—I do! I can remember 'em like the back of me hand! He wus a big feller, wus our dad! Big as a church!"

"You're a liar—you're a liar! And you'll burn in hellfire!" chanted Jubilee, while Young Nick, who'd a temper on him like boiling hot potatoes, jumped up and down with rage.

"I'm not—I'm not!" he screeched, clenching his fists till his knuckles showed almost white. He'd have smashed in Jubilee's pretty, smirking face if he hadn't been frightened of spoiling her looks, which would have meant he'd never get her wed and off his hands.

This business of getting Jubilee wed was a real worry, and had kept Young Nick awake for many a long night under hedgerows, in cowsheds and barns, and even way back in the orphanage in Kilkenny before they'd run away. It worried him sick—for how could he make his way in the world with her round his neck and weighing on his heart like a sack of turnips?

He scowled at her, sitting in the twiggy shadows of the night. What a sight! Hair like a spider's nightmare and a family of beetles going to church across her dirty dress. No self-respect. And ignorant, too. Couldn't cook, couldn't sew, couldn't read nor write. Who'd wed such an article with nothing but the skin she stood up in and a pair of gold earrings, thin as a rat's whisker, that a tinker's wife had given her, back in Ireland?

"For your dowry, dear!" the tinker's wife had said, after Jubilee had got over screaming at having her ears stuck through with a needle. "Husbands is like trout, so you'll need to bait your hook with something tasty and bright!"

"She wouldn't catch more'n an old boot!" thought Young Nick gloomily as Jubilee twisted an earring round and round in her grubby ear and gave a crafty smile.

Suddenly her eyes glittered. *"Bluebottles!"* she whispered. And she didn't mean flies!

Through the thick and bushy dark of the wild side, a lamp came swinging, like a wandering, glaring eye. Then bulky figures with gleaming silver buttons, like shillings in a dream. Policemen!

Silently, brother and sister sank into the shadows of their hawthorn home. They were frightened of bluebottles worse, even, than of bad weather. And with good cause. Young Nick in his time had done enough thieving to have been locked up for the rest of his life, and Jubilee had been a receiver of enough stolen property, in the way of sausages, puddings, and pies, to have been locked up for even longer.

But they weren't the only thieves in the world that night. The bluebottles were after another one. And as they tramped about in the grass, on feet as big as cowpats, their lamp kept poking and peering and reaching out into the dark like the long yellow arm of the law.

There were two of them, and they'd got a fat gent in a chimney-pot hat with them, who'd just been robbed of his gold watch and chain. An ugly ruffian had come up to him and asked him for the time.

"That's an old trick, sir," says one of the bluebottles.

"Heard it in me cradle, sir," says the other, swinging his lamp heart-stoppingly across Young Nick and Jubilee's hawthorn, but looking the other way. "You took out your watch and before you could say 'Jack Robinson!' he was off with the time, your watch, and all! Am I right, sir?"

Chimney Pot nodded. "Solid gold," he sighed, "and with a diamond in the back. Worth a hundred guineas if it was worth a penny!"

"I expect it's in Devil's Acre by now, sir," says the first bluebottle, and gave a little shiver.

"True enough," says the other, with a shiver of his own. "That's where it'll be."

"Best thing to do, sir," says the first bluebottle, "is to offer a reward."

"Reward?" shouted Chimney Pot, suddenly flying

4

into a rage and shaking his fists. "What for? Do you suppose the scoundrel will bring it back to me and wait to be locked up?"

"Come, come, sir!" says the other bluebottle, very calm and quiet. "There's no sense in losing our temper as well as our watch. If you was to offer a handsome reward, of, say, fifty pound, it's a sight more than he'd get from a fence."

"Fence? What the devil would be the use of a gold watch to a fence?"

"Receiver of stolen property, sir," explained the bluebottle. "Very old expression."

"Heard it in me cradle," said the other. "Very mean people, fences. Wouldn't offer him more than five pound."

"Hm!" says Chimney Pot grimly. "At least it's a comfort to hear that the robber gets robbed too!"

"Yes, sir, very comfortable indeed. So you can see, sir, that if you was to offer fifty pound, he'd be tempted."

"It's an old trick, sir," said the other bluebottle. "But it often works."

"He'd be that foolish, Constable?"

"Thieves ain't clever folk, sir."

"Save at their trade," put in his friend.

"He wouldn't come of himself, of course, because he'd know you'd recognize him."

"Recognize him? I'll say I'd recognize him! As long as I live, I'll never forget his ugly face!"

"There's many an ugly face in this town, sir,"

murmured the first bluebottle. "And one looks very like another. Was there nothing else, sir?"

"He was a Welshman, Constable."

"Ah! That's better! Taffy was a Welshman, Taffy was a thief. Taffy came to my house and stole a leg of beef!"

"Which in your case, sir," said the other bluebottle, very polite, "was a gold watch with a diamond in the back, and a gold chain."

"And you think he'll be tempted by fifty pounds?"

"I do indeed, sir. He won't come of himself, like I said. He'll send a friend, maybe even a child."

"It's an old trick, sir," said the other bluebottle. "But we'll be on to it, sharp as knives."

"We'll post a notice up in Devil's Acre, where he'll be sure to see it," said the first bluebottle.

"In Devil's Acre," agreed the other. And they both shivered again.

"Very well, Constable," said Chimney Pot, pressing his hand to his empty weskit pocket. "It's a deal of money, but it'll be well worth it if you catch the man. And not just to get my watch back! I'd pay out twice as much just to see that scoundrel put behind bars for the rest of his life!"

"FIFTY POUND!" whispered Young Nick to Jubilee when the bluebottles had gone. "What do you say to that?"

But Jubilee was fast asleep. As usual, it was Young Nick who was left to lie awake and worry about getting his sister wed. Fifty pound! And somewhere in Devil's Acre! If only he could lay his hands on that gold watch, he'd have enough to buy Jubilee a husband in almost any market!

Chapter Two

THERE WOULD HAVE BEEN ROAST DUCK for Sunday breakfast, if Jubilee had been able to cook. But she couldn't, so the fat ducks in the park waddled about on the rushy banks beside the lake with their necks unwrung. Instead, the hungry brother and sister, when they'd rubbed the sleep out of their eyes, the spiders out of their hair, and the beetles out of their rags, took their battered tin cup and made for the cows that grazed on the green and gave milk at a ha'penny the half pint.

Not that they had a ha'penny between them. As folk said, they were worse than animals: no manners, no learning, and no money. All they had was an empty cup and empty stomachs.

There were minders beside the cows, radish-faced girls sitting on three-legged stools and picking their noses while they waited for business in the way of nurserymaids, smart soldiers, and children with china cups.

"Ready!" says Young Nick, creeping up behind a cow as big as a house. "Steady—GO!" And he gives Jubilee a great shove.

She flew through the air like a tipsy butterfly, flopped down in the grass, and began jerking and squealing like a brandy fit on St. Patrick's night.

"Leastways, you're good for something," says Young Nick, crawling under the cow while its minder, who was as thick in the head as the cow itself, gawped at Jubilee going through her antics. "Even though it mayn't get you wed!"

Quick as a flea, he grabs an udder and tugs away with all his might, taking care to hold his tin cup close, so as to muffle the whoosh and the ping as the milky rush came down and foamed and bubbled over the brim.

By the time the minder stopped gawping and found out she'd been robbed, it was too late. The robbers were halfway out of the park and going like the wind, so there was nothing to be done but to thump the cow for being such a fool as to give milk without being paid.

Young Nick and Jubilee never stopped running till they'd crossed over Great Peter Street and the park was no more than a leafy green memory. Then they leaned up against a wall to catch their breath, and finished off the milk that hadn't been spilled.

"Don't lick a hole in it!" said Young Nick, at last managing to get the cup away from Jubilee and tying it onto a piece of string that served him for luggage carrier and belt. "We got to go and look for your dowry!"

Of course there wasn't a chance in a thousand of their finding the gold watch, but then they were worse than animals and couldn't count. So Young Nick took Jubilee firmly by the arm and pulled her round a corner and into the stinking muddle of alleys and lanes, of crazy old houses where folk lived like rats, sometimes as many as ten to a room, where the smells were so bad that birds flying overhead turned giddy and faint. Even the sun went green when it looked down on Devil's Acre.

It was soon after nine o'clock, and the dazed air was staggering under the booming and banging of the bells of Westminster Abbey—for Devil's Acre was right next door to God's front yard. In fact, you could have heaved a brick out of the Abbey and hit the Devil right in the eye—if he'd happened to be on his property at the time instead of sitting in Parliament and making the laws.

"Bluebottles!" squeaked Jubilee, and once again she didn't mean flies, even though there was a shining festival of them round the rubbish heaps and following the skinny, scavenging dogs. She meant the policemen from the park. They were nailing up a notice on a public-house door. One of them was banging in the nails with his truncheon, while the other was keeping watch. Apart from them, there wasn't a living soul in sight.

Presently they finished and went off together,

swinging their truncheons in time to the pealing of the bells. No sooner had they gone, than the broken-down doorways and the black holes between the houses came alive with the ragged folk who'd vanished when the bluebottles had come.

Inquisitively they crowded round the notice, scratching their heads and grinning in mystification until a scholar obliged by reading it out to them. He was a boy, a thin, scrubbed-looking boy in a blue coat, yellow stockings, and enough brass buttons to light up a street. A button-nosed, sandy-haired boy with a voice that kept going squeaky as he tried to make himself heard above the racket of the bells.

It was all about the watch. Gold, with a diamond in the back. Great sentimental value. Fifty-pound reward payable on its being brought to the police station in Rochester Row.

The crowd stood listening, nodding its head wisely, while Young Nick and Jubilee peeped and peered from face to face. They were looking for the ugly one that Chimney Pot in the park had sworn he'd never forget for as long as he lived.

There were potato noses and chins that stuck out like moldy boots; there was a plentiful crop of twisted ears and a fair sprinkling of eyes as white as milk; but there wasn't anybody really ugly . . . leastways, not in Young Nick and Jubilee's book.

"Can you tell us the time, mister?" began asking Young Nick, remembering the old trick the bluebottle had heard in his cradle, and thinking he'd know the watch if he saw it, even if he didn't know the ugly

11

face. But nobody knew the time and nobody cared. In Devil's Acre, time stood still, till you were clapped in your coffin and that was the end.

Little by little the crowd drifted back into the holes and doorways, and even the notice disappeared. Somebody had stolen it, either for decoration or kindling, or filling a hole in a boot. Nothing remained outside the public house but the boy in the blue coat and a queer-looking old fellow with skinny shoulders and a head cocked on one side, like a parrot that was several sizes too big.

"A wonderful piece of reading, Smudgeon, my boy," he was saying, smoothing down the scholar's blue coat and fingering his brass buttons with a long and bony hand. "I never heard better, not even in the valleys and chapels of Wales!"

A Welshman! Young Nick's heart beat fast!

"Your ma and your dad must be very proud of you," went on Parrot Face, his fingers lingering round Smudgeon's biggest and brightest button—till he saw Young Nick and Jubilee. Instantly his fingers ran away from the button like a grandfather spider in a fright. He cocked his head on the other side.

"There's a pretty lass," he said, with an eye on Jubilee's earrings, and giving her an enormous wink. "In a year or two, and with a good scrubbing, she'll be breaking hearts like eggs!"

"Mirrors, more like it!" said Smudgeon, and grinned all over his face.

If Jubilee had been six inches taller, she'd have given them both a clout round the ear, but she wasn't, and tried to run away. But Young Nick, with her dowry on his mind, held on to her tight.

"Can you tell us the time, mister?" he asked. And his heart jumped into his mouth as Parrot Face's fingers went to his pocket for what Young Nick knew in his bones was a gold watch! It was an old trick, but like the bluebottle said, it often worked. Or it would have done if Smudgeon hadn't spoiled it!

"It's half past nine!" he piped up. "I can tell by the bells! Ain't I right, Mr. Owen, to the very tick?"

"Right like you always are," nodded Mr. Owen, cocking an ear as the bells died away. "You're a clever lad and no mistake!" And his fingers ran away from his pocket like they'd been burned!

"Time I was going to church, Mr. Owen," said Smudgeon, with a holy smirk. "Mustn't be late."

"Say a prayer for me, Smudgeon, my boy," said Mr. Owen, laying a hand on the scholar's shoulder. "And say it right."

Off went Smudgeon, smart as ninepence. And if Jubilee had been six inches taller, he'd have gone a sight smarter, with her boot up his backside. But she wasn't, so she fell over instead.

"Come on!" said Young Nick, dragging her up to her feet. "We'll give him something to pray about!"

"Right round his earhole!" said Jubilee.

"Right round his slimy chops!" said Young Nick.

"And right up his backside!" said Jubilee, who was as mad as a wasp.

Chapter Three

Along the sunday streets went smudgeon, his blue coat swinging, his brass buttons shining, and his neat little legs going like a pair of yellow scissors, snip, snip, snip!

"Right round his earhole!" panted Jubilee, clutching half a rotten fish she'd snatched off a dog on a rubbish heap, and six yards behind.

Young Nick shook his head. Too many folk in between them and Smudgeon. She'd be wasting her fish. If she'd been six inches taller, it would have been all right, but she wasn't, and he told her so. They hurried on.

"Right round his slimy chops?" pleaded Jubilee, swinging her fish like a bluebottle's truncheon, and her eyes shining bright, like chipped glass on a wall.

"Wait till he gets to the corner," muttered Young Nick, "and then we'll let him have it, right up his—"

But before he could say another word, vengeance

was taken out of their hands! Round the corner of Tothill Street, like a rattling storm of hail, came a swarm of boys in green!

They stopped, and so did Smudgeon. And you could tell from the back of his neck that his face had gone as white as the paper on the public-house door. Fiercely Young Nick dragged Jubilee into a doorway. Vengeance was the greencoat boys—they would repay!

"Bluecoat!" grinned one, showing all his teeth. "Dirty little bluecoat boy!"

"L-leave me alone!" stammered Smudgeon, trembling all over. "P-please leave me alone! I—I'm g-going to ch-church!"

He held up his prayer book as if to defend himself, but it weren't no good. The greencoats held up prayer books of their own: they were just as holy as him. And that wasn't all. Their stockings were just as yellow and their faces were just as Sunday clean. But they wore green coats and he wore blue, and that made all the difference between peace and war and life and death.

They took a step towards him; he took a step back, and ended up against a wall.

"Bluecoat scab!" jeered the grinner with the teeth, and poked Smudgeon in the belly so that he squealed and doubled up. "Get out of our way!"

"Bluecoat rat!" said another, and punched Smudgeon in the eye. "Get out of our street!"

He howled and went down, and in a moment the greencoats were on top of him in a furious struggling heap. There was a snarling and yelping and grunting, as if Smudgeon was being torn to pieces by hungry dogs, and Young Nick wouldn't have been surprised if all there was left of Smudgeon was a couple of brass buttons and a rag of blue.

Suddenly there came a warning shout: "Look out! He's coming!" Instantly the heap grew still. Then, like a cloud of green flies rising from a meal, the boys abandoned their prey. They picked up their prayer books, put on their caps, and streamed after a stern-looking gent in black who had just appeared. Two by two they marched away, to sing hymns in St. Margaret's Church, leaving Smudgeon motionless in the dust and dirt.

"Come on," said Young Nick to Jubilee, as Smudgeon twitched and groaned and began to struggle to his feet. "We can't do no better'n them!"

He tried to pull her away, but Jubilee had been stoked up for too long to have gone off the boil. She couldn't help it. There was Smudgeon, staggering to his feet, and there was she, still clutching her fish! It seemed only natural to use it. With a screech of excitement, she flew at the tottering Smudgeon and clouted him about the head and shoulders and wherever else she could, with every last scrap of her strength!

If she'd been stronger, she'd have broken every bone in his body, but she wasn't, so she broke his spirit instead. Smudgeon burst into tears. He'd lived through the attack of the greencoat boys and was just thanking God it was over, when out of nowhere had come a screeching fury, hitting him like mad with a lump of rotten, stinking fish! It was more than flesh and blood could stand. He wept and howled and wished he was dead.

"You didn't ought to have done it," said Young Nick, dragging Jubilee back from the sobbing, cowering bluecoat boy. "She didn't ought to have done it," he explained to Smudgeon. "Not after them others had had such a go."

Smudgeon agreed. He bent down to pick up his prayer book, and Jubilee, red as a cherry, picked up his cap. It was a horrible sight, and so was Smudgeon. His face, his hair, and his fine blue coat was a ruin of dirt and stinking fish slime. He looked down at himself, and tears as big as silver onions came wobbling down his cheeks.

"They'll kill me!" he moaned. "They'll skin me alive!"

"Who? Them green ones?"

"No. The school . . . and me mum and dad!"

"What for?"

"Me coat! B'longs to the school. Now they won't have me no more. Me mum and dad'll skin me alive! Look at it!"

"It ain't so bad," mumbled Jubilee, scowling down at her feet rather than at what she'd done. "Just give it a rub and a wipe and it'll come up like new."

Young Nick stared. It was the first time in her life that Jubilee had ever thought of cleaning anything. He hoped she hadn't taken a fancy to Smudgeon. It wasn't the sort of match he had in mind for her.

"Go on," urged Jubilee. "Have a try."

17

Smudgeon shook his head. "It stinks," he said mournfully. "And it's all slimy. And it was you what did it, not the greencoat boys."

"She's worse'n an animal," confided Young Nick to Smudgeon, just to put him off in case he fancied Jubilee.

Jubilee's scowl grew black as thunder; then suddenly the sun poked through. She gave a crafty smile, and twisted an earring in her filthy ear.

"Come on!" she said. "I'll get it clean for you. I'll wash off the slime with some water from the lake in the park where we live."

Smudgeon looked doubtful. Jubilee's smile made him think of foxes and suchlike thieving things.

"You'll run off with it," he said. "Won't you!"

Jubilee shook her head till her hair flew out like a black bush in a gale. Smudgeon sniffed and wiped his puffy eyes.

"All right," he said with a sigh. "After all, I ain't got much more to lose, except for me skin and bones!"

"Then you ain't no good for Jubilee," said Young Nick to himself. "It's prospects and property what I'm aiming for, not skin and bone!"

Chapter Four

THEY WALKED TOGETHER, NEARLY: the brother and sister hand in hand, and Smudgeon half a yard behind. He was ashamed of his foxy, ragged companions, and even more ashamed of himself. And quite right too. He stank. It wasn't his fault of course—it was Jubilee's fish. All the same, folk passed him by with disgusted looks.

At last they reached St. James's Park. Being residents, they scorned the public gate and went in through a private hole in the railings, on the wild side. Then, while Young Nick and Smudgeon, in his white shirt and daffodil legs, squatted down inside the creeping, crawling, beetle-and-spidery cave of ivy and hawthorn, Jubilee bundled off to the lake with Smudgeon's blue coat.

"She'll come back?" asked Smudgeon anxiously, itching a thousand itches and not knowing where to scratch. "Won't she?"

"If she wants to get wed," said Young Nick, setting a toppled wood louse on its frantic feet.

Smudgeon looked puzzled, so Young Nick explained about his trouble with Jubilee and her dowry, and getting her off his hands.

"Good idea!" said Smudgeon, who'd never heard of a dowry before. "Wouldn't say no to getting wed meself, if there was property in it!"

"Not to Jubilee, you won't!" thought Young Nick sharply. "She goes where there's property, else I'd never get no sleep!"

"She's been a long time," said Smudgeon, uneasily.

"No more'n a flick of a cow's tail," said Young Nick, poking a twig at a ladybird to remind it to fly away home. "Why? What's the hurry?"

"Got to get me clothes back to the school."

"Far to go?"

"Chapel Street. Blewcoat School. B.L.E.W., not B.L.U.E. of course!"

"What do you mean?"

"Blew! Like—like the wind!"

"But it's Blue, ain't it? Like—like flowers!"

"Course it's blue!"

"Then why did you say it was like the wind?"

"Because the gent who started it was a bad speller. That's why!"

"Not much of a school, then!"

"Best in London!" said Smudgeon, with a burst of pride. "In the world, too, I shouldn't wonder! The Greencoats is dirt to it; and so's the Gray!"

"But it was them greencoats what smashed you up," pointed out Young Nick, shrewdly. "Weren't it!"

"That's because I was on me own!" cried Smudgeon. "If there'd been two of us, we'd have wiped the street with 'em!"

Young Nick thought about it.

"What's it like at your school? What do they learn you?"

"Oh, things . . . like reading, writing, 'rithmetic . . ."

"What's that?"

"Adding up and taking away. Money, mostly. Then, when we've learned everything, we gets apprenticed to a trade, so we've got prospects."

Young Nick squinted carefully at the boy with prospects. He shook his head. Not good enough. He was aiming higher for Jubilee.

"Do they learn girls, too?" he asked curiously. Smudgeon nodded. "What do they learn 'em?"

"Cooking, sewing, and Bible, mostly."

"Do they give 'em blue coats?" Smudgeon nodded again. "And yellow stockings?"

"Dunno," said Smudgeon. "Never seen 'em. Dresses come right down to the ground, mostly."

Young Nick frowned. Thoughts were running through his head as quick as money spiders, and when Jubilee came back, all tangle-haired and breathless, he peered at her with more than ordinary interest.

"Look!" she cried, holding up Smudgeon's coat. "Good as new!" Which was a dirty lie, as she'd never been near enough to anything new to know what it looked like! But still, it weren't bad, considering. She'd got rid of most of the slime, and what she hadn't was spread so thin it hardly showed.

Smudgeon took his coat and privately counted up the buttons.

"They're all there!" said Jubilee indignantly, and Smudgeon's ears blazed up like poppies.

"Got to be going," he mumbled uncomfortably. "Me friends'll be coming back from church by now."

"We'll come with you!" said Young Nick, standing up with a rush and a rustle of beetles and twigs. "Me and Jubilee."

"What for?" asked Smudgeon suspiciously. There was a green glitter in Young Nick's crooked eyes that made him think of the other one, Old Nick.

"We'd like to have a look at your school," said Young Nick. "Best in the world, ain't it? Besides," he said, as Smudgeon wasn't looking pleased, "we got to look after our coat, ain't we! Them greencoats might be waiting, and us two could wipe the street with 'em! Just like you said."

They left the park together, nearly: Smudgeon hurrying on in front, and Young Nick and Jubilee never letting him out of their sight.

"Small, ain't it!" said Young Nick as they came to the Blewcoat School. "You sure it's the best one in the world?"

Smudgeon nodded vigorously. "The best things is always small," he said, and for the first time in her life, Jubilee was pleased that she wasn't six inches taller.

The best school in the world was neat and square, with white-painted windows and red brick walls. It was like a mansion that was still an infant, with railings all round to stop it running out into the street to play.

Cautiously, Smudgeon looked up and down Chapel Street for a sight of his friends returning from church, but the only boy to be seen was a wooden boy, standing bolt-upright on a shelf over the school front door, a bluecoat boy with a painted coat and a varnished face.

"SMUDGEON!"

Smudgeon, who'd just opened the squealing iron gate, jumped a yard in the air. He looked up, but it wasn't the wooden boy who'd shouted, it was a terrible female from a house next door. She'd spied him out of her upstairs window, and in a moment her head had vanished and she herself had come out in the street, in a buzzing whirl of ribbons and beads, like a shiny black swarm of bees.

"WHY WEREN'T YOU IN CHURCH?" she screeched, rushing upon Smudgeon and seizing him by the ear.

"I—I was took queer!" howled Smudgeon, trying to follow his stretched-out ear before it came off. "Honest, Mrs. Rummer! I was took queer!"

"Taken! Taken!" shouted Mrs. Rummer, jerking on Smudgeon's ear like it was a bellpull and nobody at home. "Poor Mr. Rummer might as well be teaching blocks of wood for all the good it does! *Taken*, not took!"

23

Then she saw Young Nick and Jubilee standing outside the railings and looking in.

"What are you doing here?" she demanded, letting go of Smudgeon and clutching her beads, for there was something about Young Nick and Jubilee that made her think of cats and magpies and suchlike untrustworthy things. "Go away, you horrible ragged pair! Go away!"

"But we brung him back, missus," said Young Nick. "Me and Jubilee."

"Brought! Brought!" shouted Mrs. Rummer; then she shook her head in irritation. "Oh! What does it matter! You don't belong here so why should I care how you speak? So you brought Smudgeon back. Well, what have you been up to?"

She stared hard at Young Nick and then at the limp-eared Smudgeon, and her deep knowledge of boys told her that she'd never get the truth out of them in a month of Sundays, which would have taken her into the middle of next year.

"Don't tell me," she said, and looked up at the painted wooden boy over the door. "If only they were all like you!" she sighed. "Quiet, clean and never telling lies." She turned back to Smudgeon. "All right, my lad," she said. "You can go and put your coat back on its peg. How's your ear?"

"Better, Mrs. Rummer, thank you kindly."

"Hm! It's sticking out. Remind me, next time, Smudgeon, to pull the other one. It's best to have two alike."

She chuckled as Smudgeon scrambled up the steps

and vanished into the school. Then she turned to Young Nick and Jubilee.

"Are you still here? I thought I told you to go away!"

"If you please, missus," said Young Nick, holding on to Jubilee, who wanted to run away as Mrs. Rummer frightened her badly, "how much do it cost to go to your school?"

"Nothing. It's a charity school. Now, go away."

"We was just wondering, missus," said Young Nick conversationally, as if nothing short of a boot or a bluebottle would shift him, "if me and me sister Jubilee could come and be learned things in your school?"

Mrs. Rummer, who was tall and thin, and with a face like badly crumpled paper, looked at the ragged pair strangely.

"What manner of things do you want to learn, my lad?"

"Cooking, sewing, and Bible, mostly, for Jubilee, missus."

"And for you?"

"Oh, reading, writing and—and taking away money, missus."

Mrs. Rummer smiled—and it was a queer sight. All the lines in her face got deeper, like she was going to split open and there'd be another Mrs. Rummer inside.

"Well, my lad," she said, "you go home and tell your father to come and see Mr. Rummer at the school at nine o'clock in the morning. You've got a father, I suppose?"

"Course we have!" said Young Nick. "He's a big feller, is our dad. Big as a church!"

"You're a liar, you're a liar!" chanted Jubilee, before she could stop herself. "And you'll burn in hellfire!"

"WHERE ARE WE GOING NOW?" asked Jubilee as Young Nick pulled her along the street.

"Where do you think!" said Young Nick. "We're going to find ourselves a dad. The sooner you learn cooking, sewing, and Bible, the sooner I'll get you wed!"

"Let's wait for Smudgeon," said Jubilee, looking back.

"No property," said Young Nick. "He's worse'n an animal. I ain't wasting no dowry on him!"

Chapter Five

WHEN YOU GO SHOPPING FOR A DAD, you got to be careful. You don't want any old rubbish.

"There's one!" cries out Jubilee, darting like a grubby dragonfly.

"No good!" says Young Nick, dragging her away from the first dad she'd clapped eyes on, who turned out to be a dismal ruin in a tattered red jacket, standing on a street corner and holding out a hand for charity. "Only got one leg."

"But he's a soldier," pleaded Jubilee, her eyes wet and green as seaweed as she thought of bedtime stories from a dad who looked like he'd had more adventures than he'd had hot dinners.

"Too short," says Young Nick, giving Jubilee a great heave that nearly took her off her feet. "Like I keeps telling you, our dad wus a big feller, big as a church."

"You're a liar," began Jubilee, when she sees an

old bootlace seller, with black spectacles, like horrible injuries, and a shriveled-up rat of a dog. "What about that one?" And she pats her knee and makes squashy kisses at the dog.

"No good!" says Young Nick. "Got the mange. Both of 'em." And he gives Jubilee another great heave so that she vanishes down an alleyway in a whirl of legs and tatters. "We'll be best off trying in Devil's Acre!"

He was nobody's fool, was Young Nick. He knew that when you go shopping for a dad, or anything else for that matter, you got to cut your coat according to your cloth—which, in Young Nick and Jubilee's case, wouldn't have amounted to enough for a gnat's wes-kit. You got to try the bottom end of the market, where there's always a chance of picking up a bargain among the damaged goods and rubbish.

There were plenty in Devil's Acre, and a fair sprinkling of mums besides, snoring in doorways, squinting out of broken windows, and propping up the tottering public house. Sunday and the hot weather had brought them out, along with a mad mob of flies.

"It's a dad we're after!" said Young Nick sharply, and pulled Jubilee away from a skinny duchess with butterfly eyes and grasshopper legs, who'd called her "dearie" and said she was a pretty little thing and were them earrings real gold? "Mrs. Rummer said, send your dad!"

So they poked about among the dads, peering into the doorways, looking in at the windows, and leaving no battered hat unturned, to see what was dozing underneath.

"Here's a good 'un!" cried Jubilee, caught like a candled moth by a crumpled-up button-seller with a box of china buttons clutched in his lap.

"No good!" said Young Nick. "He's nothing but skin and bone. You needs to be careful when you're choosing a dad. After all, ours was a big feller—"

"I know, I know!" wailed Jubilee, suddenly losing all hope. "Big as a church! I hate churches! They're hard and cold and dark! And if that's what our dad was like—which is a dirty lie!—I'm glad I can't remember him!"

Then she burst into tears, for she'd really set her heart on the china buttons, which would have made her look as smart as a magpie.

"Look!" cried Young Nick, trying to take Jubilee's mind off her miseries and quieten her down. "Over there!" He pointed to a tipsy old hat with a loose-flapping lid—such as bats might have flown out of—that was gently snoring on a heap of old clothes. "Let's see what's under that one!"

Jubilee shook her head. She was worn out from looking, and her head was filled to bursting with the faces of dads who might have been.

"Go on!" urged Young Nick, giving her a shove. "Take a look!"

Jubilee sniffed, and brightened up. After all, it might be a birdseller, or a dad with ribbons, or even an organ-grinder with a monkey underneath the hat. She wiped her nose and eyes on the back of her hand

and tiptoed over to the snoring hat. Gently, she lifted the lid. Instantly, she shrieked and dropped it like it was boiling hot! Under the lid had been a glaring eye that had given her an enormous wink!

"It's him!" she screeched. "Old Parrot Face!"

"Looking for somebody in particular, lass?" inquired Mr. Owen, standing up and shutting the lid of his hat. "Or just for a friendly face?" He tipped his hat roguishly on the side of his head, like a parrot going to a party, and reached out a bony finger to tickle one of Jubilee's earrings.

"Oh, no, you don't!" shouted Young Nick, snatching Jubilee back before she lost half an ear as well as half her dowry. He knew what that finger was up to. Taffy was a Welshman, Taffy was a thief! "Them earrings is fixtures," he said.

"Sharp," said Mr. Owen, not in the least put out. "Sharp as pickles." He studied his disappointed finger, then rubbed it up and down the side of his great beak of a nose, as if to sharpen it up for next time. "That's what I like to see: a lad who's sharp as pickles."

"Can you tell us the time, mister?" asked Young Nick, thinking of the gold watch and the fifty-pound reward, and thieving old Parrot Face behind bars for the rest of his life. "Please?"

"Pickles and mustard," said Mr. Owen, nodding his head. "And pepper, too, I shouldn't wonder." Then, for a moment, it looked like the old trick was going to work after all. "The time, did you say?" he murmured, and his hand went to his weskit pocket.

"Why, it's—" he began, then he stopped. "Why, it's Smudgeon!" he cried, and his hand dropped away from his pocket like a spider on a broken web!

Smudgeon! He seemed to have been put on earth just to stop Jubilee getting wed!

"Well, if it ain't my little washerwoman!" cried Smudgeon, coming out of a hole between two houses like a deathwatch beetle, and just about as welcome. Or at least, it sounded like Smudgeon, even if it didn't look like him. Gone was the smart blue coat, gone were the bright yellow stockings. In their place were the coarse and shabby rags of a common street boy. Jubilee stared, and you could tell that she didn't fancy him without his brass buttons.

"Go jump in a lake!" she said, proud as a bush in May.

"After you!" said he, with a stare at her dirty legs. "And don't forget the soap!"

If she'd been six inches taller, she'd have clouted him round the ear. But she wasn't, so she whirled like a windmill while Smudgeon asked Young Nick what he was doing back in Devil's Acre.

"Looking for a dad," said Young Nick, and there was a general melting away of the loafers in the sun. Nobody wanted a pair like Young Nick and Jubilee, not even if they'd been given away with a sack of potatoes.

"What for?" asked Smudgeon. Young Nick told him about Mrs. Rummer and his hopes of school. Smudgeon thought deeply. "What about him?" he said, jerking a thumb towards old Parrot Face, who'd retired a little way off and was leaning up against a wall. "You could do worse."

"But our dad wus a big feller—" began Young Nick, outraged.

"The best things," said Smudgeon, with a knowing look, "is always small," and Jubilee smirked in triumph as at last the big feller was taken down a peg.

"Mr. Owen!" called out Smudgeon.

"He ain't no good!" cried Young Nick desperately, but it was too late. Parrot Face had looked up, cocked his head on one side, and eased himself away from the wall.

"What's your pleasure, Smudgeon, my boy?" he inquired, shuffling up close. "A song or a recitation?"

"Not me," said Smudgeon. "Them." And he pointed to Young Nick and Jubilee.

"Hm!" said Parrot Face, taking a good look. "Salt and vinegar. Well, let's see if we can sweeten 'em up!"

Smudgeon nodded and folded his arms, as if in expectation of Mr. Owen doing something wonderful, like producing roast beef and carrots from up his sleeve.

"Let's go!" muttered Young Nick, giving Jubilee a pull, but she was fixed as firm as park railings. If there was roast beef and carrots up Parrot Face's sleeve, she wasn't going to miss it. But all he had was an old tin whistle, which he polished up on his coat. Then he put it to his lips and blew a shower of notes, ending up in a bit of a tune.

" 'The Ash Grove'!" cried Smudgeon. "Let's have 'The Ash Grove'!" And Mr. Owen obliged.

He put aside his whistle and took a deep breath, which swelled him up like a bullfrog. Then, with a roll of his eyes and a clutch at his weskit, he turned from parrot into nightingale!

"Down yonder green valley,

"Where streamlets meander," he warbled, in a wonderful sweet voice that came out of him as warm and surprising as milk from a cow.

"When twilight is fading, I pensively roam . . ."

He wasn't a big feller, but he'd a voice on him twice his size—you could have heard it in Kilkenny! And all the ragged folk of Devil's Acre came creeping out of dark holes and doorways, and poking out of windows, to listen to old Parrot Face's song.

"He ain't no good!" whispered Young Nick fiercely to Jubilee. But he might as well have talked to a tree. Like everybody else, Jubilee had ears only for old Parrot Face's song.

"Ye echoes, oh tell me, where is the sweet maiden," sang Mr. Owen, with a roll of his eyes towards Jubilee, who went pink with delight.

"She sleeps 'neath the green turf down by the Ash Grove."

He stopped, and there was a great sigh, like a wind across fallen leaves. Then heads disappeared from windows, and the ragged folk crept away . . . just in case Mr. Owen had a mind to pass round the hat.

"That was a real treat, Mr. Owen," said Smudgeon proudly, and Mr. Owen nodded his over-size head. Then he turned to Young Nick and Jubilee, and examined them with care.

"That's better," he said. "Sugar and spice!"

35

"They need a dad," said Smudgeon.

"We don't, we don't!" cried Young Nick.

"We do, we do!" shouted Jubilee.

"What for?" asked Mr. Owen, judging that feelings was pretty well equally divided, and turning to Smudgeon for a deciding vote.

Smudgeon told him. Mr. Owen nodded, and there weren't no telling if it was on account of Jubilee's earrings or if he'd been took queer with a sudden kindness.

"Can't do no harm," he said, "if it's just to be their dad for a morning. Meet me outside the schoolhouse," he said to Young Nick and Jubilee, "at nine o'clock sharp."

"Lend us your watch, then!" cried Young Nick with a last desperate hope.

"Sharp," said old Parrot Face with a grin. "Sharp as pickles!"

Chapter Six

NINE O'CLOCK ON MONDAY MORNING, said the bells of St. Margaret's and St. John's. The streets were hot and crowded and the sun was high. And so was Mr. Owen.

"He's been boozing!" said Young Nick as their dad for the morning came looping along Chapel Street, with his hat over one eye and the other one rolling, like a parrot coming back from a party. "Like I told you, he ain't no good!"

"Dutch courage," explained Mr. Owen, pulling up outside the school and nearly falling over from the suddenness of his stopping.

"But I thought you was a Welshman," said Jubilee, twisting an earring round and round in her dirty ear.

"Only when I'm sober," said Parrot Face, holding on to the railings and fumbling for the catch of the gate. "Needed a drop of Dutch courage. Never been a dad before."

"He's only our dad for the morning," muttered Young Nick, keeping a sharp watch on Parrot Face's thieving fingers and the gold in Jubilee's ear.

The iron gate swung open with a squeal and a groan, and the wooden boy over the door looked like he'd got a bad smell under his nose as Mr. Owen began to climb up the steps, one by one. He were in a bad way. At last he got to the top and stood swaying, like a caterpillar looking for a leaf. Then he saw the brass door-knocker and his eyes bulged. You could tell from the back of his head. He looked round, as if to make sure nobody was watching. He reached for the knocker, but before he could nick it, it was snatched out of his grasp as the door jumped open and out poked Mrs. Rummer's crumpled face.

"I thought I heard the gate!" she cried, then shouted back over her shoulder: "They're here, Mr. Rummer! The pair I told you about! They've come with their father!"

At once, the little mansion shook and trembled! There was a banging and clattering, as if there were wild cart horses inside, and in a moment the windows were piled high with faces, staring and grinning and poking out their tongues!

"Back to your places!" came a stern voice. "This instant, I say!" and the faces vanished even quicker than they'd come. "Mrs. Rummer!"

"Yes, Mr. Rummer?"

"Keep them at it while I step next door!"

Mrs. Rummer looked up at the wooden scholar over the door. "If only they were all like you!" she sighed. "Neat, tidy, and never leaving your place!" Then she disappeared into the school just as Mr. Rummer came out of it. One moment it was her, and the next it was him. And you wouldn't have known the difference, save in the article of skirts and trousers, and Mr. Rummer's face being even more crumpled, as if it had been squeezed up for longer, and in a harsher fist.

"Owen!" cried Parrot Face, introducing himself to Mr. Rummer without being asked. "Christmas Owen!" And he took off his hat and bowed so low that Mr. Rummer had to put out a hand to stop him falling over. The big feller would have turned in his grave if he wasn't in it and could have seen the dad who was filling his boots!

"I—" began Mr. Rummer, but Mr. Owen was too quick for him.

"And there," he cried, waving his hat towards Young Nick and Jubilee, "are my chicks! They need education, sir! They need improving, sir! They need polishing, sir! They need—"

"They need washing!" said Mr. Rummer, at last getting a word in, but he didn't get no more as old Parrot Face's Dutch courage was coming out of him in a rush!

"Of course they need washing, sir!" he roared, following Mr. Rummer down the steps. "And feeding, sir, and clothing, sir! And reading, sir, and writing and arithmetic and Bible, sir! But human flesh, sir, and human blood can only do so much, and one pair of hands just ain't enough!"

39

"But what of their mother, Mr. Owen?" Mr. Rummer slipped in when old Parrot Face stopped for breath.

"Their—their mother, sir?"

"Yes, Mr. Owen, their mother."

Mr. Owen opened and shut his mouth. But nothing came out of it, save a stink of gin. He looked wildly at Young Nick and Jubilee, as if they'd come out of an egg and never had a mother at all. Then he pulled himself together, which weren't easy, considering how far he was apart. "Ah! Their mother!" he cried, and clutching at his weskit, burst out into song!

"She sleeps 'neath the green turf down by the Ash Grove!"

You had to admit it! There weren't no getting the better of old Parrot Face!

"Our dad!" whispered Jubilee proudly.

"But only for the morning!" warned Young Nick.

"That's a fine voice you have, Mr. Owen," said Mr. Rummer, after saying how sorry he was to hear that Mrs. Owen was dead and buried. "You should come and sing with the boys in church."

"Then take my chicks!" cried Mr. Owen instantly, and seized Mr. Rummer by the sleeve. "And I'll fill your church with song!" and he winked at Young Nick and Jubilee as if to say, Show me the dad who could do better than me!

Mr. Rummer thought it over. "That's a fair enough offer, Mr. Owen," he said at length, freeing his sleeve and making sure his buttons were all there. "Come into my house with your—um—chicks, and we'll see what can be done."

40

He led the way to the house next door, which was rosy red and covered in creeper, like a house playing hide-and-seek in a bush. And all the while Mr. Owen never stopped talking nor trying to nick anything shiny that caught his eye . . . not even inside Mr. Rummer's house and in his private room, with himself sitting down at his desk, with a pen in his hand and a great book open in front of him, and looking up like a tired old badger coming up for air, and just waiting for Mr. Owen to run out of breath!

"Handsome establishment, sir!" said Mr. Owen, gazing round the walls.

"Belongs to the school," said Mr. Rummer, moving a silver-plated inkwell out of Mr. Owen's reach.

"Noble profession, sir," said Mr. Owen. "Future of the nation in your hands."

"But not much else," murmured Mr. Rummer, with his eye on a silver penknife that had moved mysteriously to the edge of his desk. "Names?"

"Names?" repeated Mr. Owen, taking off his hat and scratching his bushy gray head.

"Names, Mr. Owen. What are your children's names?"

Their dad for the morning opened his mouth—

"Young Nick!" said Young Nick.

"Jubilee!" said Jubilee.

And Mr. Owen agreed.

Mr. Rummer dipped his pen in the ink and scratched them down in his ledger. Then he looked up.

"Ages? How old are your children, Mr. Owen?"

"Ten!" said Young Nick.

"Nine!" said Jubilee.

And Mr Owen agreed.

Scratch—scratch—scratch!

"And where do you live?" asked Mr. Rummer, looking straight at Young Nick and Jubilee.

"Number two, Union Court!" said Mr. Owen.

And Young Nick and Jubilee agreed.

Mr. Rummer looked at them queerly for a moment, but he scratched them down all the same. Then he put away his pen and took up a printed paper.

"These are the Rules and Orders of the school, Mr. Owen," he said. "I will tell you what they are."

"Forever in your debt, sir!" said Mr. Owen, trying to slip his hat over a brass paper-knife on the schoolmaster's desk, that Mr. Rummer rescued just in time.

"He ain't no good!" whispered Young Nick in disgust. Not that he was against thieving—it was just that old Parrot Face's Dutch courage had got the better of his Welsh caution, and he weren't no good at it!

"The school," said Mr. Rummer, half reading from the paper and half looking up, for Mr. Owen was all fingers and he was all eyes, "undertakes to provide your children with an education and to apprentice them to suitable trades when they are old enough."

"Ah! Charity, sir! Though we have all faith so that we could remove mountains," said Mr. Owen, blinking at a bronze paperweight, "and have not charity, we are nothing!"

"In addition," went on Mr. Rummer, watching

the paperweight, "the school will provide each child
with one pair of shoes, one pair of buckles, one blue
coat—"

"Coat?" squeaked Jubilee.

"One gown for Jubilee," corrected Mr. Rummer.
"One dozen of brass buttons, one woolen bag, one
pair of yellow stockings, one cap—"

"Cap?" squeaked Jubilee.

"One bonnet for Jubilee," corrected Mr. Rummer,
"and one Bible."

"Princely, sir!" declared Mr. Owen, while Young
Nick and Jubilee looked at each other with suddenly
royal eyes.

"And now for your part, Mr. Owen," said Mr.
Rummer. "You must send the children to school every
day, especially on Sundays and holidays, and with
clean linen twice a week."

"Twice a week," nodded Mr. Owen, as if it was
the most natural thing in the world.

"The school hours," went on Mr. Rummer, "are
from seven o'clock in the morning until eleven
o'clock, and then from one o'clock until five."

"Until five."

"Do you have a watch, Mr. Owen?"

"Course he has!" burst in Young Nick.

"Sharp," said old Parrot Face. "Sharp as pickles.
Takes after his mother, God rest her soul!"

"Then if you will sign this copy of the Rules and
Orders, Mr. Owen, I will put your case before the
governors this afternoon." He pushed the paper
across the desk and offered Mr. Owen his pen.

"There, at the bottom. Just make your mark, Mr. Owen."

"I can sign my name, sir!" said old Parrot Face indignantly, and did so with a splutter and a flourish.

"Our dad!" whispered Jubilee, but Young Nick muttered, "Only for the morning!"

"I will call upon you, Mr. Owen," said Mr. Rummer, taking the paper from him, "to let you know the governors' decision. Perhaps this evening. You will all be at home?"

Old Parrot Face stared. He went green, either from his Dutch courage or from the horrible shock of having a visitor.

"We like to make sure our children are not running wild," went on Mr. Rummer, glancing at the paper Mr. Owen had signed. Then he looked up and said, very softly, "They *are* your children, I trust?"

"Course we are!" cried Young Nick, seeing Jubilee's chances of cooking, sewing, and Bible going down the drain. "He's our dad all right! Signed his name, didn't he!"

"Course he's our dad!" wailed Jubilee, seeing her bonnet and gown and bright yellow stockings going likewise down the drain. "You got it written down!"

"I only asked," murmured Mr. Rummer, carefully studying Mr. Owen's signature, "because the children seem Irish, and you are Welsh, Mr. Owen."

"It's their mother who was Irish, sir!" cried Mr. Owen. "God rest her soul!"

Old Parrot Face! He were a match for Old Nick

himself! You had to admit it! But Mr. Rummer hadn't done with him yet.

"There's something else that puzzles me," he said, still studying the paper. "The boy told Mrs. Rummer that his father was a big man. Big as a church, he said." He looked up. "And that's a deal bigger than you are, Mr. Christmas Owen."

"He's a liar, he's a liar!" sobbed Jubilee. "And he'll burn in hellfire!"

"Takes after his mother, sir," mumbled old Parrot Face, looking greener than ever. "God rest her soul!"

He started to back towards the door, and beckoned to Young Nick and Jubilee to follow. "Come, chicks!" he pleaded. "Time to—to go home!"

Mr. Rummer stood up. "Remember," he said sternly, and wagged a finger that was all snowy with chalk. "This evening. I will expect to find you all at home!"

"This evening, sir," mumbled Mr. Owen, trying to put on his hat but not finding his head. "At home. All—all of us, at home."

"And I would be obliged, Mr. Owen," said Mr. Rummer, holding his hand, "if you would give me back my pen!"

Chapter Seven

HE LIVED UP TWO FLIGHTS of dark and smelly stairs inside of number two, Union Court—but everybody called it Onion Court, on account of its always running over with tears. Mostly it was screaming babies to blame, but you'd often fall over folk with shiny cheeks and puddle eyes, huddled up in the hall or on the stairs. There weren't nowhere else for them to cry in private, as all the rooms was full.

Except for Mr. Owen's. Old Parrot Face had got a room to himself. It wasn't because he was rich; it was because everybody knew he'd nick the shine right out of your eye as soon as your back was turned, so it wasn't safe to share with him. It was him who'd nicked the bluebottles' notice off the public-house door. He'd got it hanging up on his wall. And it weren't the only one! He'd got 'em everywhere: over the fireplace, stuck up round his bed and even on the back of the door. There must have been stolen property up there all the way from Cardiff to St. James's Park!

"Him and his big feller!" moaned Mr. Owen, sitting on his bed with his head in his hands and blaming Young Nick for everything. "Big as a church indeed!"

"But he wus, he wus!" insisted Young Nick, who wasn't going to be parted from his golden dad—while Jubilee poked about the room, peeping under the table, peering up at the notices, and smiling her smeary smile. Of all them three in old Parrot Face's lodging, she was the only one who was happy. "Give us a song, Mr. Owen!" she kept begging. "Our dad!"

"Get out, you filthy beast!" he shouted suddenly, not meaning Jubilee but a mangy one-eared cat that had poked its ugly head round the door like it had called for the rent.

He pulled off a boot and shied it. The cat stared and vanished. "Thieving brute!" he muttered, limping and hopping after his boot, which had gone out through the open door. "He was after me dinner," he said, coming back into the room and making sure his mutton pie, that he'd left on a shelf by his bed, hadn't been interfered with.

But it wasn't there no more. Half of it was inside of Young Nick, and the rest was still going down inside Jubilee. You couldn't miss it. Her mouth was full and there was crumbs spilling out over her chin. She were always a dirty eater, and liked to take her time.

Old Parrot Face stared at them. Then he looked at a chopper that was lying in the fireplace, and you could tell he was thinking of going for Young Nick and Jubilee with it, and getting back his pie no matter where it had gone. His eyes was red as berries. But he never said nothing. Most likely he was frightened that if Mr. Rummer was to call and find his lodging all over blood and bones, he'd have the bluebottles round like rotten meat!

Suddenly he smiled, but Young Nick wasn't taken in. He'd seen that there was more to old Parrot Face than just thieving fingers and song. A fierceness had showed, that made you think of the story of the old woman in the forest who cooked children in her oven and ate them hot for supper and cold next day.

"You'd best go downstairs, chicks," he said, trying to keep his voice soft and kind, just like the old woman in the forest. "Ground floor, back. Ask for Mrs. Smudgeon—"

"Same as our Smudgeon?" asked Jubilee, wiping her mouth on her sleeve.

"His mother," said Mr. Owen. "Tell her that Mr. Owen of upstairs would be much obliged for a lend of two sacks of wood shavings till tonight." He winked. "After all," he went on, with a chuckle in his voice, "we got to show there's somewhere proper for you to sleep, my dears! We can't have Mr. Rummer, when he calls, thinking that Mr. Owen's chicks doss down on the bare boards, eh?"

The Smudgeons were respectable folk; you had to admit it. There weren't no boozing nor cursing nor fighting, such as you'd notice. They'd got all of the ground floor back, except for a corner by the fireplace

that was curtained off by a blanket, and was let to a
Mr. O'Grady and his friend, Mr. D., who wasn't no
trouble as nobody ever saw him.

Smudgeon himself was at school, and his dad was
out selling firewood in Pye Street, so there was only
his wispy little mum at home, and a screechy baby
called Parliament, on account of having been born almost in its shadow.

"So you're the pair!" said Mrs. Smudgeon, looking
Young Nick and Jubilee up and down after they'd told
her about Mr. Owen's needs. "Our eldest," she explained, patting her hair very ladylike, "what's studying at the Blewcoat School (B.L.E.W. of course!), told
us all about you." She stood up. "So it's two sacks of
shavings for Mr. Owen. Just hold Parliament, dear,"
she said, pushing the noisy bundle into Jubilee's arms,
"while I go outside and see what Mr. Smudgeon's
left."

She shuffled out of the room, and Parliament
howled fit to burst.

"For pity's sake!" came Mr. O'Grady's voice from
behind the blanket. "Can you not put a cork or a fist
in its mouth? Me friend, Mr. D.'s trying to get some
sleep!" He poked his long, bristly face round the blanket and peered at Young Nick and Jubilee. He
beamed. "So you'll be from the old country, then!"

"Kilkenny," said Young Nick. "Our dad wus a big
feller there, big as a church," and for once Jubilee
didn't call him a liar, as she was busy with Parliament.

"That's a tremendous feller, then!" said Mr.
O'Grady, with a whistle of admiration. "I'll ask me

friend, Mr. D., when he wakes up, if he was ever acquainted with the gentleman. Big as a church, did you say? And from Kilkenny?"

Then, before Young Nick could beg him to wake up Mr. D. right away, Mrs. Smudgeon came back and Mr. O'Grady disappeared behind his blanket.

"Tell Mr. Owen this is the best I can do for him," she said, holding out two limp sacks. "There ain't much in 'em, and what there is, is more chips than shavings. But as it's only for show, it don't really matter." She gave the sacks to Young Nick and took Parliament out of Jubilee's arms. As she did so, she frowned. "You want to watch them when you're upstairs, dear," she said, staring hard at Jubilee's earrings. "Meaning no disrespect, but Mr. Owen do have his little ways!"

"Did you hear that?" whispered Young Nick to Jubilee as they climbed back up the stairs.

"About our dad?" said Jubilee, meaning Mr. Owen.

"About Mr. D. and Kilkenny," said Young Nick, meaning the big feller, and his eyes were shining bright as stars.

Chapter Eight

"THAT CAT!" shouted out old Parrot Face, with a wild roll of his eyes all round his lodging.

"What cat?" asks Young Nick and Jubilee, thinking he'd gone off his head.

"That thieving, one-eared tabby brute! You must have let it in with you!"

"Never!" says Young Nick and Jubilee, angel pure.

"I can hear it scratching!"

"That's Jubilee," says Young Nick. "Got insects." Which were true, as she was always a great scratcher-out of the little things.

"Then for pity's sake, stop it! We don't want Mr. Rummer, when he calls, to think that Mr. Owen's chicks have got livestock!" said old Parrot Face, still anxiously looking round his room.

He'd been busy. While Young Nick and Jubilee had been downstairs with Mrs. Smudgeon, he'd tidied his bed, taken all the notices off the walls, and had even spread a ragged bit of carpet over the wormy floorboards in front of the fireplace.

He was very particular about the carpet and didn't want nobody to tread on it in case it got worn out before Mr. Rummer came. "Get off, get off it!" he'd shout, whenever it looked like Young Nick or Jubilee was going to put a foot wrong. Then he'd wink and grin, as if it was all a great joke. But you could tell he was worried sick over the visit and was frightened that Mr. Rummer would catch him out in something.

"Stop that scratching!"

"I weren't!" said Jubilee—which were a dirty lie, as everybody knew she was as itchy as an ant heap.

Mr. Rummer came early. He came back with Smudgeon, straight after school, still in his governor's-go-visiting black coat and shiny black hat. You never saw a schoolmaster so quick! He crossed over the yard like a long streak of ink, with Smudgeon almost running to keep up with him, and old Parrot Face only just had time to get a gulp of Dutch courage down inside him before Mr. Rummer was up the stairs and knocking on the door.

"Coming, sir!" spluttered Mr. Owen, wiping his mouth and putting his bottle back on the shelf with a shaky hand. "Coming directly!"

He rushed to open the door, and hopping backwards and bowing and parting the air in front of Mr. Rummer like he was drawing back invisible curtains, begged him to step inside.

"As you see, sir, everything is just as you wished!

We are all at home, ha ha!" (More curtains, behind which were Young Nick and Jubilee, sitting on the bed.) "Me and my chicks!" (Curtains again, this time for Mrs. Smudgeon's sacks that had been laid on the floor under the window, side by side.) "My little family, ha ha!"

Mr. Rummer nodded. "I came right away, Mr. Owen," he said, taking off his hat and gloves and putting them on the table where he could keep an eye on them, "because I have some good news for you. The governors," he said, walking over to the fireplace and standing, with his hands clasped behind his back and his beetle-black boots planted on old Parrot Face's carpet, "have agreed to take your children into the school!"

Everything was all right! Old Parrot Face tottered with relief, and Young Nick held on to Jubilee's hand as tight as he could. She really was going to be educated, improved, and polished. She was as good as wed!

"Stop scratching!" he whispered fiercely.

"I weren't!" whispered back Jubilee—which were a dirty lie again, as you could hear her at it, busy as a bedbug.

"The children," said Mr. Rummer, with a sharp look at them, as his schoolmaster's ear had caught either the whispering or the scratching, "are to commence their attendance at the school tomorrow morning, at seven o'clock."

"Seven o'clock, sir!" agreed old Parrot Face, who couldn't wait for the visit to be over and done with, now that everything was settled. "On the very stroke! My chicks will be on your doorstep, sir!"

Mr. Rummer nodded but made no move to go. He took a piece of paper out of his pocket and gave it to Mr. Owen.

"The Rules and Orders of the school," he said. "This is a duplicate of the paper you signed this morning. You are to keep it carefully to remind you of the duties and responsibilities you have agreed to, Mr. Christmas Owen."

"Like the Bible, sir!" cried Mr. Owen, immediately fixing the paper on one of the nails in the wall where his notices had been, then offering Mr. Rummer his hat and gloves. "Rules and Orders! They shall be my study morning and night, sir!"

He were a quick thinker, were old Parrot Face, you had to admit it!

"Then let me draw your attention to the first article, Mr. Owen," said Mr. Rummer, as if his hat and gloves was still on the table instead of right under his nose.

"The—the first article, sir?"

"Yes, Mr. Owen. It requires you to send the children to school in clean linen." He paused and stared sternly at the filthy pair on the bed. "In clean linen, Mr. Owen."

"C-clean linen?" stammered Mr. Owen, looking at his ragged chicks in a sudden, hopeless dismay. And Young Nick looked at Jubilee, and Jubilee looked at Young Nick, and they wondered if their kingdom was going to be lost for want of a shirt and a shift.

But it weren't, of course. It was just Mr. Rummer's schoolmasterish way of seasoning good news with a pinch of fright.

"But no matter," he said, when the fright had sunk in to his satisfaction, "Mrs. Rummer, in her great wisdom, foresaw that there might be a difficulty. She has sent a shirt for the boy and a petticoat for the girl!"

He unbuttoned his coat and brought out a brown paper parcel. He gave it to Mr. Owen, and for once, old Parrot Face didn't know what to say. His eyes filled up with tears, which were as much from gin as from warm feelings. He started to thank Mr. Rummer, but Mr. Rummer didn't want no thanks.

"A little refreshment, sir?"

But Mr. Rummer didn't want no refreshment, neither. He wanted his hat. Mr. Owen gave it to him.

"And my gloves?"

Awkwardly, Mr. Owen fished for them in his pocket, looking like he didn't know how they'd got there—which were very likely true, as thieving came as natural as breathing to old Parrot Face. He pulled them out and dropped one on the carpet. Mr. Rummer bent to pick it up. He paused, half kneeling.

"There's something scratching," he said, with a frown.

"Jubilee!" cried Mr. Owen, with a terrible look. "Always scratching! Takes after her mother, God rest her soul!"

"That's a dirty lie!" shouts Jubilee, jumping up and down. "It weren't me!"

"It's under the floor," says Mr. Rummer, listening to the carpet.

He was right. There was a mad scratching and scraping, much worse than Jubilee, coming from under the carpet. Old Parrot Face went as green as a leaf!

"Must be somebody downstairs," he said feebly.

Mr. Rummer gave him a look. It was a real schoolmaster's look, meaning, I know you're up to something, my friend, and I'm going to find out what! Next moment, he'd got the carpet pulled back and was down on his hands and knees.

"Quick, man!" he cried. "Something sharp to lever up one of these floorboards! Ah! Never mind! This will do!" He got hold of the chopper in the fireplace and began working it into a crack. "There . . . there!"

Up came the board.

"Good God!" cried out Mr. Rummer, jumping back in a fright. He was only just in time. There was a terrible hiss and a scream, and out of the hole flew the mysterious scratcher! It were in a hurry, all right. With a blaze of yellow eyes, it bolted under the bed like a puff of tabby smoke! It was the cat!

"Puss-puss!" wheedled Jubilee, bending down and making a bird of her fingers and sweeping the floor with her hair. "Puss-puss!"

But nobody took any notice. There was other things, more interesting. The cat wasn't the only article that had been hidden under the floorboards. There was a heap of scratched and torn-up paper, and peeping and winking among it, like gold and silver children playing games, was all old Parrot Face's private property!

There was watches and chains and spoons and penknives and brass door-knockers and every other bright and shiny item he'd nicked all the way from Cardiff to St. James's Park!

He'd wrapped them up in his notices as soon as Young Nick and Jubilee had gone downstairs, and had stowed them out of harm's way. But the cat had done for him. The crafty brute must have crept into the hole while his back had been turned and he'd boarded it up without knowing!

"J-just a little nest egg, sir," old Parrot Face mumbled hopelessly, as Mr. Rummer stared down sternly at his secret tickery. "K-keeping it safe for—for my chicks. B-belonged to their mother, God rest her soul!"

Mr. Rummer didn't say nothing, but you could tell he was thinking a whole Bibleful. He looked straight at Mr. Owen, who seemed to shrink into a crumpled heap of skin and perspiration. Then he looked at Young Nick and Jubilee, who was still trying to coax out the cat from under the bed. He looked round the little room and at the two sacks on the floor. He sighed and shook his head. Then, still without saying anything, he put back the floorboard and covered it with the carpet again. Old Parrot Face stared.

"Well, Mr. Owen," said Mr. Rummer at length, brushing the dust from his knees and buttoning up his coat, "I don't think I need to intrude upon you any

longer. You have the Rules and Orders and you know what is required of you." He put on his hat. "But there is just one thing I must impress upon you, Mr. Christmas Owen. If you yourself do not bring the children to school every morning at seven o'clock, I will send the police here to make sure they are all right." He looked down meaningly at the carpet, and Mr. Owen shuddered. Mr. Rummer smiled faintly. "I take it that we understand each other," he said.

Old Parrot Face nodded. He understood, all right. He was either a dad for life, or it was the bluebottles!

"Until tomorrow morning, then," said Mr. Rummer, putting on his gloves and opening the door. "You should have no difficulty in being punctual," he murmured, with another look at the carpet, "as you are well provided with means to tell the time!"

As soon as Mr. Rummer had gone, old Parrot Face tottered to the shelf and took another dose of Dutch courage, to get over his fright. Then he told Young Nick and Jubilee to go downstairs again and ask Mrs. Smudgeon if she'd be so obliging as to extend the lend of her sacks for another day or two. "After all," he said, with a mournful smile, "we can't have Mr. Owen's chicks dossing down on the bare boards!"

NIGHT IN ONION COURT WAS HOT AND SMELLY, and all shut in. It was full of sighings and moanings, sudden cries and shouts, and a broken drizzle of sobs. There weren't no owls in Onion Court, nor spooky bats, nor foxy rustlings and clicking beetles, like there was in the ivy and hawthorn cave in St. James's Park. But one thing was still the same. Just like always, Young Nick was left to lie awake alone and worry about getting his sister wed. Jubilee, curled up on her sack like a hedgehog, was fast asleep and dreaming her silly dreams, while old Parrot Face was snoring loud and regular, in his bed by the fireplace wall.

St. Margaret's had banged out midnight long ago, and misty moonshine was poking through the cracked and dirty window like a pale old lady in gloves. Young Nick peered cautiously at the carpet, and wondered about the treasures underneath. Somewhere among them was the gold watch with a diamond in the back. Fifty-pound reward.

He sighed. With fifty pound and her earrings, Jubilee would be able to get a husband in any market. She wouldn't need no schooling, so they'd be able to leave Onion Court and go back to their ivy and hawthorn home in the park. Young Nick didn't like Onion Court. He didn't like its noisy night. And most of all, he didn't like skinny old Parrot Face being their dad.

"Our dad," he whispered into his hard and lumpy sack, "wus a big feller, big as a church!"

He fell asleep, and dreamed of having a long talk downstairs, with Mr. D. behind the blanket, who'd been in Kilkenny at the time of the big feller, and had actually laid eyes on him. "Big as a church, says you?" murmured Mr. D., "Why, he wus as big as . . ." But his voice was so soft and muffled that Young Nick couldn't hear properly. Desperately he tried to pull aside the blanket. He struggled and struggled—and woke up!

He opened his eyes—and stared straight into the bulging eyes of Mr. Owen! Old Parrot Face was bending right over his chicks and staring down at them! And he was holding the chopper!

"W-what do you want?" whispered Young Nick.

"You were having a bad dream."

"W-what's that for?" asked Young Nick, staring at the chopper.

"None of your business."

The room was very dark. The pale old lady had long since wandered away. Even so, Young Nick could just make out that the carpet had been moved from the fireplace. So that was it! Old Parrot Face had been moving his property! He didn't trust Young Nick any more than Young Nick trusted him.

"Sharp," breathed Mr. Owen, seeing the direction of Young Nick's look. "Sharp as pickles!"

He started to creep back to his bed, when Jubilee stirred and woke up. She saw old Parrot Face, and smiled sleepily.

"Give us a song, Mr. Owen," she begged. "Our dad!"

He paused. Then he sighed and came and sat in the dark beside his chicks. The night was still noisy. The sighing and moaning and crying out never stopped.

"*Please!*" pleaded Jubilee.

Old Parrot Face sighed again. Then, very softly, he began to sing.

"Deep the silence round us spreading,
All through the night . . ."

Jubilee's eyes were shining better than stars, and even Young Nick had to admit that old Parrot Face had a sweet voice inside him, even though he was as skinny as winter.

"Dark the path that we are treading,
All through the night . . ."

His voice swelled, filling the little room and reaching out into the night.

"Still the coming day discerning,
By the hope within us burning . . ."

Little by little, the sighing and moaning, the crying out and the sobbing, grew quiet, as all Onion Court listened to old Parrot Face's song.

"To the dawn our footsteps turning,
All through the night."

He stopped, and Onion Court was silent and at peace.

"Our dad!" murmured Jubilee happily. Then her stars went out and she was asleep.

Chapter Nine

Seven o'clock, said Mr. Rummer—or it was the blue-bottles.

"For God's sake!" shouted Mrs. Rummer, looking out of her window and spying Mr. Owen and his little ones sitting on the steps outside the front door of the school, in clean linen. "Have you lost your senses? It's only a quarter past six!"

Next moment, she was out in the street, with her hair all screwed up in curlpapers and her face all screwed up in temper.

"But, dear lady—" began Mr. Owen, taking off his hat and bowing as Mrs. Rummer came storming up the steps.

"Be off with you!" she ordered. "Leave the children with me!"

"But, dear lady—"

"What are you waiting for? Ah! I suppose you

want to see your—your chicks in their fine new feathers, eh?"

"Dear lady—"

"Well, they'll look just like that!" She pointed to the painted wooden boy over the door. "Only they won't be so quiet! They won't be so clean! And they won't be so respectful-looking! More's the pity! Now, be off with you, my man!"

Old Parrot Face sighed, put on his hat, and with a rueful look at Young Nick and Jubilee, shuffled down the steps and trudged away. Mrs. Rummer, hands on hips, stared after him.

"Big fellow indeed!" she muttered. "Ah, well! Maybe he'll grow!" She turned to Young Nick and Jubilee, who were still sitting on the steps. "Why are you looking so down in the dumps?" she demanded angrily. "Isn't this what you wanted? Reading, writing, cooking and sewing, Bible and—and taking away money?"

Young Nick didn't say nothing; he wasn't sure anymore.

"Stand up when you're spoken to!" said Mrs. Rummer sharply. They stood up. "Now! Come along with me—the pair of you!"

She beckoned, with an iron finger, down the front steps and then down another flight at the side that led into the areaway, where there was a low, arched door, like the door of a prison.

"This is the Sinners' Door," she said, unlocking it. "It's the way in for children. All children are sinners until they learn better. That's what schools are for!"

She opened the door and a powerful smell of stale boys came out. "Into school with you!" she cried, and Young Nick and Jubilee, clutching each other tightly by the hand, crept fearfully into their strange new life.

"WELL, NOW!" cried Mr. Owen, welcoming Young Nick and Jubilee back to his lodging at the end of the day. "How was it, eh? Your first day at school!"

"We done alphabets," muttered Young Nick, not wanting to say that it had been the worst day in all his life.

It had been a day of misery and bewilderment, of drowning in rivers of words he couldn't understand, and of being pushed off his bench by the boy sitting next to him, who never got caught. It had been a day of loneliness and fright, and of living in terror for the safety of his ears, which, he found out, had been given to boys not just to hear with, but to be used as handles, like cups, when the Rummers wanted to wake a boy up. Even the fine new clothes hadn't been much comfort. They'd itched and prickled like they was full of ants and bees, and Jubilee's bonnet had made her look like one of them mushrooms you couldn't eat.

In short, it had been a bad day, and if Jubilee hadn't been sitting a hundred miles away, at the other end of the huge wooden schoolroom, and in the middle of twenty great bony, grinning girls, him and her would have made a bolt for it, back to their ivy and hawthorn home. There, at least, though they'd always been hungry, and had often been wet and cold, they'd belonged to themselves. Now they belonged to the Rummers and the Blewcoat School, just like they was sacks of potatoes or coal! Earwigs and beetles were better off!

"We done singing!" said Jubilee, forgetting that she'd cried her eyes out every time she'd gone to the bog, and skipping round old Parrot Face's room, happy as a flea. "And we had a pie with Smudgeon at dinnertime, on the corner of Horseferry Road!"

"We had a story," said Young Nick.

"So did we!" said Jubilee. "Right out of a book!"

"We done adding up and taking away," said Young Nick. "Money and things!"

"We done sewing," said Jubilee, sucking her pincushion fingers. "Look what I made!" She fished down inside the neck of her petticoat and pulled out a bit of cloth, edged with stitches as black and wobbly as a spider's legs, and speckled all over with her blood. "It's a handkerchief! I made it for you, Mr. Owen," she said. "Our dad!"

Old Parrot Face stared at it and blinked—as well he might, for it weren't even big enough to wipe a butterfly's nose, let alone his great beak.

"Well, now . . . hm! . . . think of that!" he mumbled, shaking his head in wonderment. "Hm! . . . that's really something!" He took it and tucked it into his sleeve; then, with another shake of his head, he told Young Nick and Jubilee to go down to Mrs. Smudgeon and tell her that Mr. Owen presented his compliments and would she be so kind as to oblige him with the lend of a couple of plates? "After all," he said, "we can't have Mr. Owen's chicks eating off the floor!"

"We ain't his chicks!" muttered Young Nick, as they went down the stairs.

Jubilee sniffed. "He didn't even say he liked it!" she said. "The handkerchief what I made!"

"Our real dad would! He wus a big feller . . ." said Young Nick, and for once, Jubilee didn't call him a liar.

There was just Mrs. Smudgeon and Parliament at home. Smudgeon's dad was still out selling firewood and Smudgeon himself, his mum explained, with a ladylike pat at her wispy head, had gone to the boozer for a pen'orth of pickled onions and cheddar for the family supper.

"So it's plates he wants to borrow now!" sighed Mrs. Smudgeon after Young Nick had told her. "Meaning no disrespect, but if your Mr. Owen was to give back everything that didn't belong to him, there wouldn't be enough of him left worth burying! Here! Hold little Parly for me, dear!" she said, pushing the baby into Jubilee's eager arms. Then, with a weary shake of her head, she went off into the kitchen to see what she could find.

Jubilee sat down on a chair and tried to stop Parliament's noise by singing one of the songs they'd done at school, but you had to admit she weren't as good at it as old Parrot Face. Parliament kept on drizzling worse than February.

Young Nick crept up close to the hanging blanket. His heart was beating fast.

"Mr. D.!" he whispered.

Instantly, a bristly head poked round the blanket with a startled glare. It was Mr. O'Grady.

"Who wants him?"

"It's me, Mr. O'Grady . . . from—from Kilkenny!"

Mr. O'Grady rubbed his eyes.

"Well, now! To be sure, to be sure! So it is! B'Jaysus, but that's a sweet noise!" he said, meaning Jubilee's singing. "Can she sing 'In Dublin's Fair City'?"

Young Nick shook his head. There was more important things on his mind. "Did you—did you ask Mr. D. about our dad?"

Mr. O'Grady stared. Then he clapped his hand to his head.

"Of course, of course! The big feller, big as a church!"

"That's right! Did you ask Mr. D.?"

"B'Jaysus! I clean forgot!"

"Can you ask him now?"

"He's gone out. Not five minutes ago. But I tell you what! I'll tie a knot in the tail of me shirt to remind me. Kilkenny. Big feller. Big as a church!"

Then, before Young Nick could make sure that he tied the knot, Mrs. Smudgeon came back and Mr. O'Grady vanished behind the blanket as quickly as if he owed the rent.

"Two plates," she said, giving the articles to

Young Nick and taking Parliament out of Jubilee's arms. "And my compliments to Mr. Owen, and would he be so kind as to oblige us with a lend back of the chopper he borrowed off Mr. Smudgeon last January?"

They went back upstairs. To their surprise, old Parrot Face had gone out. They were alone in his room for the very first time, and somewhere under the floorboards was the gold watch with a diamond in the back. Young Nick didn't wait. In an instant, he was down on his hands and knees, levering up the boards in front of the fireplace with Mr. Smudgeon's chopper. All he could think of was what fifty pounds could do. No more schooling . . . no more Onion Court . . . and no more old Parrot Face, who'd broken Jubilee's silly heart.

There wasn't nothing there! Crafty old Parrot Face had moved his property further off than Young Nick had bargained for. Up came more and more boards, with squeals and grunts, and down went Young Nick's head and arms into the mousy, dusty dark. He was going at it like a terrier after a rat, when Jubilee screeched, in a terrible fright, "He's coming, he's coming!"

Young Nick banged his head and swore. Then, quick as a cricket, he began hopping and jumping all over the floor, stamping the boards back into place. He'd only just finished when there was a noise on the stairs like trees falling down, and a moment later, the door burst open and in lurched Mr. Owen.

He wasn't alone. Smudgeon was right behind him,

trying to hold him up. He was a horrible sight. He'd got Jubilee's handkerchief pressed to his nose, which was pouring blood!

"I'b all right, I'b all right!" he moaned, as Smudgeon helped him onto his bed. Young Nick needn't have bothered about the floor. Old Parrot Face wouldn't even have noticed if the roof had been off.

"Boozed to the eyeballs!" muttered Young Nick in disgust, while tears ran down Jubilee's cheeks as she stared at her ruined hard work, the first she'd ever done.

"No he ain't," said Smudgeon. "He never had a drop. I was in the boozer and saw it all."

"What happened?"

"He'd come in to show everybody his new hand-kerchief that his daughter had made for him with her very own hands, and somebody, a real big gent, laughed and said it looked more like she'd done it with her feet. So Mr. Owen told him he needed his eyes washing out, and threw half a pint of beer in his face. That's when he got his wallop on the snitch. But that didn't stop him. He went for the big gent and I had to drag him out or he'd have been half killed. I never knew he had such a temper. You should have seen him! He was blazing mad over that handkerchief!"

Jubilee's face was as bright as sunshine after a shower.

"Then he *did* like it!" she cried happily, while old Parrot Face lay on his bed and groaned. "He did, he did!" She clapped her hands in delight. "Our dad!"

71

Chapter Ten

Sₘᵤ𝐃GEON TOLD EVERYBODY. The battle in the boozer got famous; even Mr. Rummer, who didn't hold with fighting and nearly pulled your ear off if he caught you, smiled and said it was lucky Jubilee hadn't made Mr. Owen a shirt if that's how he carried on over a handkerchief! He said that, from what he'd heard of the huge size of Mr. Owen's adversary, it must have been like David and Goliath, and he read it out of the Bible; but it turned out to be a dirty lie, as it wasn't the little 'un in the story what got thumped and had to be helped out of the boozer with a nose like a bee cluster that didn't go down for a week!

Young Nick burned with the shame of it, but Mr. Owen, as soon as he found out that people admired him for his spirit, swelled up, worse than his nose, with pride. He went out and got himself a new hat, a couple of chairs, a teapot, and a whole heap of clothes for his chicks. There was shirts and petticoats, shoes and stockings, a yellow dress for Jubilee and a red plush weskit for Young Nick, which, you had to admit, made him look as smart as a robin.

"Self-respect," said Mr. Owen, studying the effect of his new hat in a looking glass he'd borrowed off Mrs. Smudgeon. "We can't have Owens, even little ones, going about in rags!"

"We ain't Owens!" muttered Young Nick.

"*Aren't!*" cried Jubilee. "Mrs. Rummer says we ain't to say 'ain't'!"

Young Nick clenched his fists, but held his peace . . . even though there was war in his heart. He thought about the knot in the tail of Mr. O'Grady's shirt, that was to remind that bristly gent to speak to his friend, the mysterious Mr. D. He'd been downstairs several times, to borrow articles for Mr. Owen, but the Smudgeons had always been at home, and Mr. O'Grady never showed himself if there was a Smudgeon in sight.

Most dinnertimes, when it wasn't raining, Young Nick and Jubilee went back to St. James's Park. Old Parrot Face gave them the money for a half pint of milk and a bit of pie, so there wasn't no need to nick anything. All the same, the cow-minder had looked at them queerly at first. She left off picking her nose and scratched her head, as if, somewhere inside the respectable blue coat and gown, the smart cap and bonnet, and the bright yellow stockings, she'd recognized something thievish and foxy she'd seen before.

"Haven't I . . . ?" she muttered. "Ain't you . . . ? No! It can't be! Them other two was worse'n animals!" Then she shook her head, took the money, and filled the cups.

The leaves were beginning to change color, and so were Young Nick and Jubilee. Their weathered complexions softened, and the sharp and spiky look that came from dwelling among twigs and thorns was fading away.

"There's no more butterflies!" sighed Jubilee, peering into their old ivy and hawthorn home.

"Too cold for 'em," said Young Nick. "Summer's over and done."

"But she's still there," said Jubilee, pointing to a beady-eyed spider, crouching in a tattered web. "Remember when that other spider came a'-courting her, and gave her a fly all wrapped up in shiny stuff?"

Young Nick nodded. "But it's different for us," he said gloomily. "It's us what's got to give the shiny stuff if ever I'm to get you wed."

That night there was mutton chops for supper, with tea for Young Nick and Jubilee out of the new teapot, and nearly half a bottle of Dutch courage for old Parrot Face himself. He needed it, he said, to keep out the chill, as he had to go out to meet somebody on business, in the park.

"If you're still awake when I come back," he said, pulling on his coat, "I'll give you a song!" and he played tunes in the air with his bony fingers as they came wriggling out of his sleeves.

"I know his business," said Young Nick when Mr. Owen had left the room and gone stumbling down the stairs. "Nicking watches!"

"Thieving!" cried Jubilee. "Mrs. Rummer says we're not to say 'nicking'!"

Young Nick scowled at her. Schooling wasn't doing her no good. When you added up what was Jubilee's, and took away, like with sums, what old Parrot Face had given her, all you was left with was green eyes, a squeaky voice, and a bit of gold in her ears— same like she was before.

"You keep a watch at the window," he told her, and started searching again for old Parrot Face's property. Fifty pound was a sight more likely to get Jubilee wed than learning to talk proper.

MR. OWEN HAD GONE OUT AT NINE; at two o'clock, by the chimes of St. Margaret's, he was still out in the dark. Anxiously, Young Nick waited, listening and staring towards the door. He hadn't found so much as a teaspoon, let alone the gold watch, so he was keeping awake to spy on old Parrot Face and find out his new hiding place.

"Give us a song . . . give us a song . . ." sighed Jubilee in her sleep.

"Shh!"

Jubilee woke up.

"Where's our dad?"

"Not back yet. And he ain't our dad!"

"Isn't! We mustn't say 'ain't'! What time is it?"

"Two o'clock. Go back to sleep."

"Something's happened to him!"

"He's boozing somewhere, most likely."

"The bluebottles have got him!"

"We'd have heard."

"He's been knocked on the head in the park!"

Young Nick thought about it.

"Come on!" he muttered. "Let's go and look!" He wouldn't have left a dog to lie alone and untended in the park all night.

Small and white-faced, they rose from their sacks and got dressed—which was different from the old days when you never took nothing off so you never had nothing to put on. Soft as moths, they flitted from the room, down the stairs, and out into the night.

There weren't no moon, and only a thin sneeze of stars. Devil's Acre was as black as a hole.

"Mr. Owen! Mr. Owen!" they breathed, into every crack and slit between the houses, and they poked and prodded every heap of rubbish to make sure he wasn't lying underneath. "Mr. Owen! Mr. Owen!"

"He's dead!" wailed Jubilee.

"Not him!" whispered Young Nick, tightening his grip on Jubilee's hand. "Not old Parrot Face!" But all the same, there was a terrible chill in his heart.

The park was dark and quiet, and Young Nick and Jubilee crept shivering through the shadows, like a pair of little foxes, queerly dressed in a flickering yellow dress and a red plush weskit with buttons that winked and stared.

They were frightened in a way they'd never been frightened before. Every tree was a huge policeman, every bush was a lurking murderer, and every patch of blackness was a dead man lying in the grass.

"Mr. Owen! Mr. Owen!"

An owl shrieked, a twig cracked, leaves rustled. Young Nick and Jubilee clutched at one another. They stared about them with wild, wide eyes that had forgotten the alarms and mysteries of the night.

"Mr. Owen! Mr. Owen!"

A huge night-flying moth blundered into Jubilee's murky hair. She cried out.

"Shh!"

"I couldn't help it."

"Listen!"

There was a thin, silvery squealing somewhere in the air.

"Must be a mouse, caught by an owl!"

"Mice don't play tunes! Listen!"

It was a whistle, a tin whistle!

"Mr. Owen! Mr. Owen!"

"*Deep the silence round us spreading . . .*" softly warbled the whistle.

"*All through the night!*" answered Jubilee, shrill with joy!

"*Dark the path that we are treading . . .*" wailed the whistle.

It was here, it was there, it was everywhere!

"*All through the night!*"

It was coming from a clump of trees that grew by the lake!

"*Still the coming day discerning . . .*" sighed the whistle, almost at its last gasp, as Young Nick and Jubilee rushed among the gnarled and wrangling trees.

"By the hope within us burning . . ." pleaded Jubilee to the faint, invisible whistle. "Where are you—where are you?"

"All through the night!" came a voice at last, hoarse with fright and cold. "I'm here, chicks, up in the tree!"

They looked up. High among the branches of a spreading oak was something dark and bulky, with a pale face faintly shining down, like a fallen moon. A hand waved feebly. There was a creaking and a groaning, and a sound of tearing; then down came Mr. Owen like a windfall of rotten fruit!

"Our dad!" cried Jubilee happily.

"Why didn't you come home?" demanded Young Nick.

"Locked in," mumbled old Parrot Face. "The gates are all shut."

"You been out thieving, ain't you!" accused Young Nick.

"I—I—"

"The bluebottles was after you, wasn't they!"

"Pickles," muttered Mr. Owen, too worn out even to manage "Sharp as."

"Chased you up the tree, didn't they!"

"And mustard."

"We thought you'd been knocked on the head," said Jubilee.

"Sugar," sighed Mr. Owen, searching the ground for his hat.

"That's why we come looking for you," said Young Nick.

"And spice," said Mr. Owen, with a painful smile.

"I'm cold," said Jubilee. "Let's go home."

"But the gates—"

Young Nick and Jubilee looked at one another in wonderment.

"Gates," said Young Nick, like he was Mr. Rummer talking to his worst pupil, "is only for them what's got the keys."

Together they crept across the park towards the wild side.

"What did you get?" asked Young Nick, naturally curious.

Mr. Owen didn't answer, but it was plain from the look on his face that he'd got nothing.

"He ain't no good at it," muttered Young Nick to Jubilee as they scrambled through their private hole in the railings. "Specially after half a bottle of his Dutch courage. The big feller would—"

"The big feller," whispered Jubilee, her eyes shining as at last old Parrot Face managed to squeeze himself through the bent railings after his chicks, "would have been caught and jugged! He'd never have got through that hole like our dad!"

Chapter Eleven

T HERE WASN'T NOTHING ON THE TABLE for supper next
night, not even a bit of cheese. There weren't no
money. Mr. Owen had been caught unawares by the
landlord on the dark of the stairs and had had to pay
him the rent. It had cleaned him out, he said. And as
he'd twisted his ankle when he'd fell out of the tree,
he hadn't been able to carry on his usual line of business, which required a turn of speed.

"What about them articles what was under the
floor?" asked Young Nick. He was hungry. In the old
days when there wasn't nothing to eat, him and Jubilee just curled up and went to sleep. But now it was
different. "What about all them silver chains and
spoons and suchlike?"

"Gone," said old Parrot Face, and Young Nick felt
sick with dismay as he thought of the gold watch that
had been his best hope of getting Jubilee properly
wed.

"Where?"

"To—to some gentlemen in Pye Street."

"What for?"

"Money, of course! It doesn't grow on trees," said Mr. Owen, and shuddered. "Where do you think your dinners have been coming from, and your shirts and petticoats, your fine red plush weskit and pretty yellow gown? Where do you think the chairs you're sitting on have come from, and the blankets that keep you warm now the nights are chilly? Eh? Eh?"

He cocked his head on one side and glared at his chicks as if it was all their fault. He never said nothing about his own new hat and fancy shoes, which weren't nothing to do with Young Nick and Jubilee. Then he sighed and said they'd best go downstairs and present his compliments to Mrs. Smudgeon and ask her if she'd be so kind as to oblige Mr. Owen with the lend of half a loaf and a bit of sausage or cheese.

But there weren't no luck downstairs. Mrs. Smudgeon was sorry but she couldn't oblige with so much as a cabbage leaf. She was expecting company, she said, with a pat at her hair, and everything had gone into the stewpot. Young Nick and Jubilee sniffed the rich and steamy air, and sadly nodded their heads. Mrs. Smudgeon shrugged her shoulders.

"Meaning no disrespect," she said, wiping Parliament's nose with a dishcloth, "but it's Owen by name and owin' by nature, ain't it! What about them plates he borrered?" Then she sighed and said that if Young Nick and Jubilee would be good enough to present her compliments to Mr. Owen and tell him that if he'd be kind enough to oblige her with a lend back of her plates, and a lend of his chairs, him and his little ones would be very welcome to join the family meal.

"I only mention the chairs," she said, "because Mr. Smudgeon's chopped up our last this very morning. The firewood business," she explained, "is a terrible breaker-up of hearth and home. Why, he can hardly look at anything—even in church!—without saying, 'That'll chop up a treat!' It's a wonder we've still got a door! Remember, now!" she called out as Young Nick and Jubilee rushed off with the good news. "There's company, so I'll need them plates!"

YOUNG NICK HAD HOPED that the company would include Mr. O'Grady and Mr. D., but they was only lodgers so they stayed behind their blanket and never showed their faces, not even after the stew.

The company was a friend of Mr. Smudgeon's. Young Nick and Jubilee had often seen him about Chapel Street and in the park. He was a blind gent who played the big drum, the triangle, the bells, the pipes, the tin plates, the spoons and the hurdy-gurdy in the street—and all at the same time! He'd got everything hung all over him, so there wasn't no part of him that wasn't musical. Everybody called him Whirling Willy, on account of the jerking and twisting and jumping about he had to do when he was rendering a tune.

"It's a gift!" said Mrs. Smudgeon admiringly.

"That it is, ma'am," said Whirling Willy, who was

sitting on the floor with his feet stretched out straight in front of him and resting up against his big drum, which he'd got strapped on, like a tremendous thump-back. "I won't deny it."

"Brings in a tidy sum," said Mr. Smudgeon, picking up the hurdy-gurdy and examining it with interest. "Mind you, this would chop up a treat!"

"Sometimes I can take as much as nine or ten shillings in a day," said Whirling Willy, reaching out a blind hand for his hurdy-gurdy before Mr. Smudgeon forgot himself and chopped it up. "Your 'Bluebells of Scotland' is always a good earner, and of course your 'Home, Sweet Home.'"

"Really!" said Mr. Owen. "You surprise me, sir! I'd have thought, with all your brass and percussion, you'd have gone in for something more stirring, like the 'Men of Harlech'!"

"That was Mr. Owen," explained Mrs. Smudgeon, as Whirling Willy turned his screwed-out eyes towards the new voice. She was always very helpful with the blind gent, even when he didn't need it. "He's from upstairs. His little ones are studying at the Blewcoat School (B.L.E.W., of course!) like our Smudgeon. Mr. Owen's a very musical gentleman too."

"You don't say!" said Whirling Willy, wagging his head at Mr. Owen so that the bells on his queer little tin hat pealed out like a moth's wedding. "Always agreeable to meet a fellow artist! Concertina, bagpipes, or pianner organ, maybe? Your pianner organ's a good earner, that is, if you've got a monkey. Brings in as much as five shilling a day, if it don't rain!"

"Vox humana, sir," said Mr. Owen. "The human voice."

"Ballad, Italian opera, or comic song, might I be so bold as to ask?"

"Ballad, sir."

"Ah! Your ballad's a good earner, specially where there's drinking going on!"

"I don't perform professionally, sir. I sing for the love of it."

"And very nicely too," said Mrs. Smudgeon.

"Are you in the firewood line, then?" inquired Whirling Willy, shifting his legs so that the tin plates that were tied to the insides of his knees clashed together. "Like our friend Mr. Smudgeon, here?"

"I'm in—er—business," muttered Mr. Owen, going a bit red. "But I'm thinking of giving it up. Too much running about, if you know what I mean."

"Then why not try a bit of the Tommy Tucker," suggested Whirling Willy. "Sing for your supper, eh? A good ballad'll bring you in a couple of shillings a night, I shouldn't wonder! That is, of course, supposing you've got the lungs for it!"

"Oh, he has, he has!" cried Mrs. Smudgeon, and Jubilee poked her nose in with "Give us a song, our dad!"

"Ah! You can't deny the ladies, Mr. Owen!" said Whirling Willy. "You'll have to give 'em a song! And tell you what! As it's by special request of the ladies, I'll perform alongside of you!"

"Thank you. Thank you, but—"

"All I need to know is, are you high or low? I don't bother with all them sharps and flats and things! Just say if you're high or low!"

"I sing tenor, sir, high tenor. But I can go down in the valleys if it suits your convenience."

"Are you familiar with 'The Bluebells of Scotland'?"

"I'd be happier with 'Men of Harlech,' sir."

"A noble tune, but it ain't really your good earner. Your best earners are them what tugs at your heartstrings and brings on your tear. If I might put it professionally, Mr. Owen, a bit of silver in the eye puts a bit of silver in the hat! Might I be so bold as to suggest 'Home, Sweet Home'?"

Mr. Owen agreed, so the blind gent held out his arms and, with a grand jingling of his bells, was helped to his feet.

"Give me room!" he cried, hooking himself up to his drumstick and triangle. "Just keep me from falling into the fireplace, that's all I requires. Otherwise give me room! For when I'm rendering, the devil gets into me! Are you ready, Mr. Owen?"

"Ready, sir!"

"Right! Now I starts off with three wallops on me drum, which, to put it professionally, we calls your Over Chewer. Then it's every man for himself!"

Mr. Owen swelled up, everybody crowded back, then Whirling Willy thumped three times, and they was off!

It were a tremendous sight! There was old Parrot

Face, clutching his weskit and near bursting his lungs, all about roaming through pleasures and palaces where there weren't no place like home, while Whirling Willy jerked and jumped and kicked and puffed like a grandfather grasshopper what was musically inclined!

"It's a gift!" marveled Mrs. Smudgeon, snatching Parliament up off the floor and out of harm's way. Then she looked up at the cracked ceiling, the filthy bulging walls, and at the faces shining all round her, thin and sharp as knives, and wiped a tear from her eye as old Parrot Face sang, sweet and high:

"Be it ever so humble, there's no place like home!"
and blind Whirling Willy clashed and whistled and jingled in joyful agreement.

"What did I tell you!" demanded Whirling Willy, when the song, the "Well dones!" and the "Wonderfuls!" was over, and he'd shaken hands with Mr. Owen and all the folk from Onion Court who'd crowded into the passage, thick as bees, had drifted away. "Ain't it your good earner?"

"It is indeed, sir!"

"Tell me now, and tell me straight! Did we draw silver, or did we not?"

Mr. Owen looked round the room. Tears as bright as sixpences stood in the Smudgeons' eyes.

"We drew silver, sir."

"Sixteen shilling, that would have brought in, up in Piccadilly," said Whirling Willy, nodding his head and unhooking himself. "Maybe even a pound, if we was to have given 'The Bluebells' as well! That would have been eight shilling for you and twelve for me, on account of me greater skill and your Over Chewer, of course. Think of it, Mr. Owen! Eight shilling in a single day!"

Mr. Owen thought about it.

"That's a fine instrument your musical gent has, ma'am," said Whirling Willy to Mrs. Smudgeon, after thanking her for supper and hoping he'd repaid her handsomely by his rendering. "Mind you, when he said he was vox humana, I was doubtful, as I've always considered your pianner organ to be a better earner!"

"Ah! The pianner organ!" sighed Mr. Smudgeon. "Now, that would have chopped up a treat!"

"But I must admit, I was took by surprise," said Whirling Willy, being guided to the door. "By the volume and power of his vox humana, he must have a chest on him like a barrel! Your Mr. Owen must be quite a big fellow!"

"He ain't! He ain't!" cried out Young Nick, who couldn't keep quiet any longer. "He's only a shriveled-up little thing, not much bigger'n a weasel!"

But he was too late. Nobody heard him. They'd all gone outside, even Jubilee, hand in hand with Smudgeon, to help guide the blind gent on his right way home. Young Nick was left alone in the room, his heart aching with anger on behalf of the real big feller he remembered from long ago in Kilkenny.

"Mr. D.! Mr. D.!" he whispered, creeping up to the blanket.

"Why, if it ain't me little friend from the old country!" came Mr. O'Grady's voice, and round the blanket came Mr. O'Grady's head.

"Is Mr. D. awake?"

"You don't think he'd be sleepin' through all that din!"

"Then—"

"Of course he'd be awake if he was here! But he ain't. Gone to Liverpool. Went not five minutes before you came in. Back in a couple of days."

"Did you—did you remember to ask him about the—the big feller?"

Mr. O'Grady scratched his tufty head.

"That I did."

"And what did he say?"

"Well, now, I've got some good news for you, and some bad! The good news is, that he thought he remembered the big feller, though he couldn't swear to the exact size of him next to a church."

"And—and the bad news?"

"He couldn't remember his name. It was on the tip of his tongue, he said, but he couldn't quite manage to shake it off! But not to worry! he said. He'd got a friend up in Liverpool with a memory as long as your arm! So you can set your heart at rest, me boy! Mr. D. will be back with that name in a couple of days!"

"Do you promise?" pleaded Young Nick. But Mr. O'Grady had vanished, as he'd heard the Smudgeons coming back.

"What a wonderful evening!" sighed Mrs. Smudgeon, rocking Parliament in her arms. "Who'd have thought we'd have had Mr. Willy and Mr. Owen rendering together, just for us alone!"

"They ought to be proud of their dad," said Mr. Smudgeon, with a nod towards Young Nick and Jubilee, "them young Owens!"

"We ain't Owens!" cried Young Nick.

"Oh! And what are you, might I ask?"

"I'll tell you," muttered Young Nick, "in a couple of days!" And everybody laughed.

Chapter Twelve

Next night there was mutton chops on the table. And that weren't all! There was boiled potatoes, pickled onions, a dish of cabbage, and a lump of cheese as big as old Parrot Face's hat!

"He's been at it again," muttered Young Nick to Jubilee, round the side of a mutton chop. "Nicking things in the park!"

"Sharp!" says old Parrot Face, all over winks and grins. "But not sharp enough!"

It turned out he hadn't been nowhere near the park. He'd joined up with Whirling Willy and had been singing his heart out in Piccadilly and Leicester Square! He kept chuckling and rubbing his hands together, like it was something wonderful what he'd done—which, you had to admit, it were, as it wasn't everybody what could sing alongside a professional gent in places like Piccadilly and Leicester Square!

"What did you sing?" asked Jubilee.

"What did you earn?" asked Young Nick.

"We rendered 'Home, Sweet Home' and 'The Bluebells of Scotland,' of course, as they're your best earners. Then we went on to 'Cockles and Mussels' and finished up with 'The Ash Grove.' "

"And what did you earn?" repeated Young Nick.

"Twelve shillings in the hat, which was seven for him and five for me."

"He said you should have got a pound if you done 'The Bluebells' up in Piccadilly!"

"And so we would if the bluebottles hadn't moved us on because of stopping the traffic!"

"I wish we could have heard you!" mumbled Jubilee, having a go at the cheese. "Give us a song now! Go on, our dad!"

Old Parrot Face shook his head. His voice was all wore out, he said, and now it was an earner, he had to take care of it.

"Won't we never hear you sing anymore, our dad?"

Mr. Owen thought about it.

"Tell you what," he said at length. "I'll have a word with my partner and ask if he has any objection to Mr. Owen's chicks having, what we'd call professionally, complimentary tickets for Saturday and Sunday nights!"

But Whirling Willy didn't like it, and said so. He didn't hold with children. They was worse'n animals, he said. He wouldn't trust them near money in a hat any further than he could see them. And everybody knew how far that was!

"Them's my sentiments," he finished up. "So I leaves it to you, Mr. Owen, always bearing in mind that what the eye doesn't see, the heart doesn't grieve over. Much!"

Mr. Owen respected the blind gent's feelings. On them Saturday and Sunday nights when Young Nick and Jubilee crept along to listen to him and Whirling Willy rendering outside public houses up in Piccadilly and Leicester Square, he never said nothing about them, not wanting to cause any grieving.

"Children?" he'd ask, all surprised, when they got too close and the blind gent sniffed and muttered something about "worse'n animals." "What children, sir?"

But Whirling Willy knew all right!

"If you asks me," he said to Mr. Owen one bad night when there wasn't much in the hat. "There's been children about! And children, Mr. Owen, for all their fine Blewcoat schooling, is generally better at taking away than they is at adding up!" He fingered over the money again. "Two shilling and a ha'penny!" he said, shaking his head with an angry jingle. "We done your 'Home, Sweet Home,' and we done your 'Bluebells,' and all we've got is two lousy shilling and a ha'penny in the hat! There ought to have been more, Mr. Owen, there ought to have been more! Them two items, as well you know, have always been good earners!"

"But it's foggy, sir," explained Mr. Owen. "There's just not the folk about. Why, you can't even see across the street!"

He were right. It were a real thick night, with the street lamps slopping about in it like broken eggs.

"Can't see across the street, eh!" shouted out Whirling Willy, and he shook all over with laughing! "Fancy that, now! Well! you'd best stay close to a blind man, what's better used to the dark! Let's go on to Leicester Square, where there's always folks about!" Then he shouted, "Just follow the blind man!" and he set off like it was clear as day!

The fog got real bad round Haymarket, and you couldn't hardly see your feet. Folk was calling out and blundering into one another like shadowy great moths—and all the time, Whirling Willy was laughing fit to burst!

"Follow the blind man!" he kept roaring out as he jingled and thumped along. "Fog don't make no difference to him!"

He were as happy as a king, and you could hear him banging and clashing away in the soupy black, and sometimes giving a turn on his moaning hurdy-gurdy just to cause a fright.

"Follow the blind man! Follow the—"

He never got no further. There come a rolling and a clattering, then a screech and a howl and a tremendous great bang!

"What's that?" cries out old Parrot Face, with a terrible roll of his eyes; then off he rushed into the fog, with Young Nick and Jubilee flying after, hand in frightened hand!

It were him all right, it were Whirling Willy what had howled and banged! He was lying in the street like a bit of old rubbish, all tangled up with his hurdy-gurdy and drum. He'd been knocked down by a cab what had been blinder than him!

Folk was crowding round, pushing and shoving for a better look, while the cabdriver kept saying it weren't his fault, and tried to quieten his horse what was rattling and screaming with fright.

"I know him, I know him! He's my partner!" shouted Mr. Owen, but a gent what said he was a doctor told everybody to keep back and called for some light.

Lamps was fetched, off the cab and out of a public house, and made a great yellow fuss in the night. Then the doctor got down next to Whirling Willy, with faces floating all round him, like pale bits of bread in soup, while the cabdriver never stopped saying that it weren't his fault.

"Aha!" says the doctor, poking at Whirling Willy and feeling him all over. Then he says "Oho!" and "Hum!"—while Young Nick and Jubilee crawled about among the shuffling feet, trying to collect what had come off Whirling Willy when he'd gone down.

"Here's his pipes!" shouted Jubilee.

"And here's his triangle!" cried Young Nick. "But it's all bent!"

"Hush, chicks!" warned Mr. Owen. "You know his sentiments! If he hears children, it'll make him worse!"

Then the doctor got up, put on his gloves, and said that Whirling Willy would have to be took off to hospital as he'd broken his leg.

"It weren't my fault!" said the cabdriver. "He was right out in the middle of the street! Crazy old fool! He should have looked where he was going!"

"But he's blind!" said Mr. Owen, and everybody cried "Oh!" and "Poor old devil!" and the cabdriver didn't know where to put himself for shame!

Whirling Willy was moaning, so Mr. Owen bent down and give him a dose of Dutch courage to ease him of his pain.

"Have we got a good crowd, Mr. Owen?" he mumbled, after his lips was wiped. "Just answer me that!"

"Close on a hundred."

"Then pass the hat round, before they gets away!"

He were a real professional gent, you had to admit it! And old Parrot Face weren't far behind.

He did wonderful well, and what with the cabdriver starting things off with a gold half sovereign, he come back with close on fifteen pound in his hat! It were the best him and Whirling Willy had ever done!

"Your broken leg's a good earner all right," groaned Whirling Willy, as he was lifted into the cab what had offered to take him to hospital free of charge. "But I wouldn't recommend it, Mr. Owen— not above your 'Home, Sweet Home'!"

NEXT DAY they went to visit him in the hospital, and he looked all shrunk and shriveled up without his instruments on, like a withered old nut come out of its shell.

"Children ain't allowed, Mr. Owen!" was his very first words from his iron bed of aggravation and pain.

"What children, sir?" asks old Parrot Face, respecting the blind gent's well-known feelings.

"Oh pardon me, pardon me!" says Whirling Willy, sinking back. "I forgot that on Saturdays and Sundays, Mr. Owen, you always walks on three pair of feet!"

"I've brought your money, sir," said Mr. Owen, trying to cheer him up.

"Not so loud!" muttered Whirling Willy. "I ain't alone in here!" And he jerked his head towards the bed next to him, where there was another gent with his leg bandaged up, like Whirling Willy's, as stiff and white as a tree in winter.

And he weren't the only one! The huge room was full of moaning gents, lying in long iron rows, with their arms and legs hoisted up on ropes, like dancing dolls what had suddenly stopped when Mr. Owen and his chicks had come in.

"Ten pound for me," mumbled Whirling Willy, counting out the money and laying it down on the bed, "and four pound nineteen shilling for you, Mr. Owen."

"But it's all yours, sir! After all, it was your leg!"

"Ah! But it was your hat, Mr. Owen! Besides, it'll be three month before I'm on me feet again and rendering, so you'll be on your own. And though I don't like to mention it, you've got extra pairs of feet what'll need feeding!"

"That's very kind of you, sir!"

"Professional, Mr. Owen, just professional. And if you'll take my advice, you'll get yourself a pianner organ for ten shilling a week up in Clerkenwell. Your vox humana is all very well, but it's subject to your damp and your chill and gets hoarse, Mr. Owen, which is something what never happens to your pianner organ! Of course, it would be a better earner if you had a monkey, but maybe one or other of them extra pairs of feet could help out with a bit of dancing."

Old Parrot Face looked at Young Nick, who shrugged his shoulders, and then at Jubilee, who gave a little hop and a skip.

"Maybe so, sir," sighed Mr. Owen. "Maybe so!" and he give a feeble wink at his chicks.

"Do me a favor, Mr. Owen!" says Whirling Willy of a sudden. "Me ten pound! I won't be needing it here. I'd be obliged if you'd take it away with you, and keep it safe!"

"Are you—are you sure, sir?" asked old Parrot Face, looking mighty uncomfortable, which weren't to be wondered at considering how famous he was for what Mrs. Smudgeon always called "his little ways."

"Of course I am!" said the blind gent irritably. "I ain't simple, you know! I knows when I can trust a man! I goes by the look in his voice!"

Young Nick and Jubilee stared at Whirling Willy like he was mad, and then at Mr. Owen as he put the blind gent's money away in his pocket.

"I'll keep it safe for you, sir," said old Parrot Face. And then, catching sight of Young Nick's and Jubilee's stare, he murmured, "I promise!" and there was tears in his eyes.

Just as they was leaving the hospital, they met the cabdriver coming in with a bag of grapes, what must have cost him a night's work.

"For the blind man what was knocked down last night," he said. "But it weren't my fault!"

Chapter Thirteen

Jubilee cried her eyes out; and it weren't on account of the blind gent having broke his leg! It was because old Parrot Face broke his word.

"You winked!" she sobbed.

"I never did!" says he.

"You did, you did! You winked at us when Mr. Willy said you was to get a pianner organ so we could do a bit of dancing in the street!"

"There—there was a speck of dust stuck in my eye."

"It's a dirty lie!" wailed Jubilee, who'd set her heart on doing a bit of dancing up in Piccadilly and Leicester Square.

Old Parrot Face shook his head. There wasn't going to be no dancing because there wasn't going to be no pianner organ. There was just going to be him, his tin whistle, and his vox humana.

It didn't do him much good. First time he tried, he

only come back with a shilling and sixpence, and his voice was wore out to a rag.

"Mr. Willy said your pianner organ never gets hoarse," said Jubilee, all puffy-eyed.

Mr. Owen didn't deny it, but he'd made inquiries and it turned out that your pianner organ was subject to other infirmities. It was always getting filled up with dust and dirt and going out of tune, what cost money to be put right. Then there was the silk in front, what cost two shillings a yard and never lasted more than a month. And where would they keep it? It was a large article and would have to be kept downstairs in the hallway, where it would have been a terrible temptation for Mr. Smudgeon to chop it up a treat!

But Young Nick and Jubilee knew in their heart of hearts that them weren't the real reason. He didn't want no pianner organ because he didn't want his chicks interfering in his business in a professional way.

"The big feller," whispered Young Nick to Jubilee in the middle of the night, "would have gone up to Clerkenwell and come back with your pianner organ right away! *He'd* have had us dancing up in Piccadilly from now till Kingdom Come!"

But just like always, Jubilee was fast asleep.

Next morning, on the way to school, she had another go. They was waiting to cross over Chapel Street when, all of a sudden, she hops off the curb and does an Irish jig, panting out the tune in her squeaky voice and jumping up and down as fast as a flea!

Folk stopped and stared, and some of them clapped their hands in time, but if Mr. Owen hadn't snatched her out of the way of a cart, she'd have ended up next to Whirling Willy, with her legs up in the air on ropes, doing a dance what never moved!

"Don't you ever do that again!" he shouted, and started her off crying worse than before. Then he turned on Young Nick, as if it was all *his* fault for not holding on to Jubilee tight.

"But it would have been a good earner!" sobbed Jubilee. "Folk liked it and clapped! If only we had a pianner organ—"

"And if only we had a monkey that could do tricks!" sighed old Parrot Face, getting over his temper and fright. Then he come out with it. "No, chicks," he said, with a shake of his head. "Dancing and singing just isn't for you. I know you're both clever at reading and writing and sewing and Bible, but rendering before the public's another matter. It's professional. You—you just ain't musical enough, and you'd spoil me pitch!"

But that night, after he'd eaten his supper, he had to eat his words!

Soon after seven o'clock, there come a knock on the door.

"Must be one of the Smudgeons!" says Mr. Owen with a sigh, for they was always coming up for a lend back of something or other. "Come in, come in!"

The door opened, but it weren't no Smudgeon what walked in! It was Mr. Rummer, in his best black coat and hat!

He gave everybody a terrible fright! Mr. Owen went as white as his new teapot, and so did Young Nick and Jubilee!

"W-what have th-they done, sir?" asks old Parrot Face—which was only natural, as why else should the schoolmaster have come to Onion Court at seven o'clock of a winter's night unless it was to tell Mr. Owen that his chicks had been found out in a crime?

Mr. Rummer never said nothing. Being a schoolmaster, he was used to causing a fright, and liked to make the most of it. He stood, staring at the floor by the fireplace, where Mr. Owen's property had once been hid; then he looked round at the new furnishings, and lastly at old Parrot Face himself, who was over by the table with his arms round Young Nick and Jubilee, as if he'd have fallen over if they hadn't been there to hold him up.

"What have they done, Mr. Owen?" says Mr. Rummer at last, taking off his hat and gloves. "Well, now, as today is Monday, they've done reading and writing and one or two sums. The girl has done needlework and cookery, and the boy, I'm sorry to have to tell you, had to stand in the corner for talking during prayers." He paused and frowned. Then he went on, "And of course, as it's Monday, they've done music."

"M-music, sir?"

"Yes, music, Mr. Owen. And that's why I'm here."

Then it all come out. It were about Jubilee. It turned out that she had a good ear—and it weren't nothing to do with its being valuable on account of the gold earring what she wore in it. It was because she was natural in music.

Mr. Cage, what played the organ in St. John's, and who came to the school on Mondays, Wednesdays, and Fridays, had found it out. He'd told Mrs. Rummer, who'd told Mr. Rummer, who'd felt it his duty to come and tell Mr. Owen.

"Yes," he said, looking at Jubilee, who couldn't stop beaming with pleasure and pride. "The child is musical, Mr. Owen."

"Takes after her father, sir!" said old Parrot Face promptly—and only just stopped himself saying "God rest his soul!"

"She should be encouraged, Mr. Owen," said Mr. Rummer, looking round the room again. "It's a pity she has no instrument at home."

"Instrument, sir?"

"Yes, Mr. Owen. She has shown a remarkable aptitude for the violin."

"And—and the boy, sir?" asked old Parrot Face, with a quick look at Young Nick.

But it turned out that the boy didn't have no genius for music, even though, Mr. Rummer admitted, he was much cleverer than his sister. He was wonderful quick at figures. In fact, he had a real genius for arithmetic, which, you had to admit, was just as good as music!

Then Mr. Rummer, after reminding Mr. Owen of his promise to sing with the boys in church, put on his hat and gloves and went away.

"Well!" said Mr. Owen, pouring himself out a dose

of Dutch courage. "It looks like I'll have to eat my words! One of my chicks really is musical!" He shook his head and sighed. "The violin, eh? I'll have to ask my partner if your violin is a good earner!"

He didn't lose no time. Next afternoon he was in Chapel Street, waiting for Young Nick and Jubilee to come out of school. He'd had a stroke of luck, he said. He'd been rendering in Queen Street and a Welsh gent had give him a gold sovereign for "Land of My Fathers" and "Men of Harlech," what had turned out to be your good earner after all.

"So we'll go and look at violins," he said, and winked. Then he remembered his last one and warned Jubilee that a wink wasn't as good as a nod, and he wasn't making no promises. Which was a dirty lie as there was fiddles shining out of both his eyes.

He'd been making inquiries, he said, and had found out that, although not to be compared with your vox humana, your violin was a tolerable earner, and that there was a shop just off Soho Square where he could get a superior instrument to them what was hanging up in the pawnshop in Pye Street.

"So let's hurry, chicks!" he cried seizing them both by the arm. "Let's get there before the shop shuts!"

It were a queer old shop, with a painted violin in the window and a real forest of fiddles inside. And when you went in and shut the door, they all hummed and trembled, like there was ghosts in the air, trying to cheer themselves up with a wispy bit of a tune.

"I want a violin," says old Parrot Face to the gent behind the counter, "for my girl here."

"Ah!" says the gent, looking down at Jubilee over the top of his spectacles. "You'll be needing a half-size."

"A good one!" called out Mr. Owen, as the gent vanished into his fiddle forest. "A superior instrument, if you please! My girl is very musical!"

"I've found one!" cried out Jubilee, jumping up and down, and pointing to a half-size golden brown fiddle what was hanging up behind glass.

"No good!" said Young Nick, pulling her away like he done when they was looking for a dad. "Too old!"

"But I want it!" shouted out Jubilee, like she done with them other dads; then the gent come back with a pair of brand-new fiddles and bows, and Jubilee took her nose off the glass and went over to the counter.

"Would the little musical lady like to try one?" asked the gent.

Jubilee held out her hands.

"Let me tune it for you first," says the gent, and plucks away at the strings and tightens up the pegs. Then he gives one to Jubilee, who tucks it under her chin, waves the bow in the air and nearly puts old Parrot Face's eye out, and starts off with a screech worse than the old cat in Onion Court.

Then she gives another couple of screeches, and starts rendering "The Ash Grove." It were as thin and high up as a bird. Old Parrot Face couldn't get over it. He kept nodding and waving his arms about in front of her, and humming alongside. She done wonderful, considering she hadn't been learning long. But you had to admit it were better when she stopped.

"Would the little musical lady like to try the other instrument?" asked the gent—which Jubilee done, but it didn't make no difference.

"There's talent there, all right," said Mr. Owen. "But of course, she's still very young."

"And so are the fiddles!" sighed the gent. "It's the bridge, you know. It always sinks on these new instruments. Consumptive, we call 'em."

"Consumptive, eh?" murmured Mr. Owen. "Well, I suppose every instrument has its infirmities, like your pianner organ and your vox humana, which is my own instrument, in a professional way. How much?"

"Three pound ten shillings," says the gent. "Including the bow and case."

"As much as that?" says old Parrot Face, going a bit green.

"It ain't a toy! It's a professional article!" says the gent—when Jubilee cries out, "I like this one best!" And she'd got her nose up against the glass again.

"Ah!" says the gent, coming out from behind the counter. "The little musical lady has a good eye as well as a good ear!" And he opens up the glass door and takes out the old fiddle as gently as if it was his own baby.

"It's an Italian instrument," he explained to Mr. Owen. "Made in Cremona a hundred and fifty years ago."

He began to tune it up, bending his ear down close. When he'd done, he looked up, and there was Jubilee staring at the old fiddle like it was a mutton pie.

"Perhaps," he said, smiling, "the little musical lady would like to try the instrument? It would be doing a kindness. These old violins, you know, love to be played. They're like you and me, sir," he said to Mr. Owen. "When they're old, they need occupation to keep 'em sweet!"

Then he give Jubilee the violin and bow, and after a scrape or two, she starts rendering "The Ash Grove" all over again. And it were very queer, what with her being only nine, and the fiddle being a hundred and fifty, how well they got on together!

It were different from them other fiddles. It were very sweet and strong, and as Jubilee stood in the middle of the room, with her fingers fluttering and trembling like white butterflies, and her face nestled into the golden brown of the old fiddle, like a flower asleep, nobody moved nor said a word.

It were something wonderful, you had to admit it. If she'd gone fishing for a husband, she wouldn't have needed no more dowry than her earrings and the old violin. She'd have caught a king!

"How much?" asked Mr. Owen, his hand in his pocket, all ready to pay.

"Fifty pounds!" said the gent, and old Parrot Face's hand come out of his pocket like it was on fire!

"Fifty pounds?" he cried, clutching his weskit with the shock of it.

111

"And not a penny less," said the gent.

"Fifty pounds!"

"Including the bow and the case. Would you like me to put the instrument aside for the little musical lady, just for a couple of days?"

Old Parrot Face looked at Young Nick and Jubilee, and then sadly back at the gent.

"For a couple of years would be nearer the mark," he sighed, and Jubilee cried her eyes out all the way home.

Chapter Fourteen

"Go on upstairs, chicks," said Mr. Owen. "There's supper waiting on the table, if the cat hasn't got there before you!"

"Ain't you coming with us?" asked Young Nick.

"I'll be up presently. I—I just wanted a word with young Smudgeon first."

Jubilee looked up at him, with soaking eyes.

"Can I come with you?" she asked.

Old Parrot Face shook his head.

"You'd frighten him to death," he said, "looking like that!"

"What do you want to tell him?"

"I—I just wanted a lend of his songbook," said old Parrot Face, and gives a wink and a clutch at his weskit, like he was going to burst out into a tune. "Don't you remember? I promised Mr. Rummer that I'd sing in church with the boys!"

Which were another dirty lie, as nobody was allowed to take books home from school—excepting the Bible, of course—and he knew it!

"Well?" says Young Nick, catching him out as soon as he come back upstairs. "There weren't no songbook, was there!"

"So it's pickles again!" sighed old Parrot Face, shaking his head. "But you're right! I clean forgot the rules!"

All through supper he were very deep, not saying much, but humming to himself and tapping his fingers on the table, like he was beating time to his thoughts. Then, when it were about half past seven, he kept getting up and looking out of the window, but as it was dark, he couldn't see much more than his own face, looking back at him as if to say, "What a queer old bird you are!"

Once he went downstairs again . . . for a breath of fresh air, he said, but he'd have needed to go a sight further than Devil's Acre to get a bit that wasn't already wore out! He just couldn't keep still, and when there come a knock on the door (it were past eight o'clock) he jumped right out of his chair!

It were Smudgeon. He was in his overcoat, and all steamy and panting from running in the night.

"I've got it, I've got it, Mr. Owen!" he cried.

"Hush, my boy!" muttered old Parrot Face. "No need to shout!"

"I did like you told me, Mr. Owen! I told them I found it in the park!"

"Not so loud, my boy, not so loud!"

"They gave me the money and didn't ask no questions at all!" said Smudgeon, and held out a little bag.

"Thank you, my boy," says old Parrot Face, taking the bag with an angel smile. "You've done very well!"

Then the bluebottles come in, them huge ugly pair from the park, big and quiet as the night!

Jubilee screamed, and so did Young Nick, but it weren't no good. Everything had come to an end!

"It's an old trick," said one bluebottle, taking hold of one of old Parrot Face's arms, "sending a child to claim the reward!"

"And it's an even older trick," said the other, taking hold of old Parrot Face's other arm, "to follow that child and catch the thief!"

It were the gold watch with the diamond in the back what had done it. Old Parrot Face had sent Smudgeon with it to Rochester Row to get the fifty pound for Jubilee's violin.

"My chicks, my poor chicks!" moaned old Parrot Face, hanging up between the bluebottles like a dead bird.

"It ain't no use crying over spilt milk," said one of the bluebottles—him what was as red as meat.

"You should have thought on them before you stole the gentleman's watch," says the other—him what was toadstool gray.

Which were the dirtiest lie of all! Old Parrot Face never had no chicks to think on when he'd nicked the watch! Him and Young Nick and Jubilee was strangers then, and wouldn't even have knowed each other if they'd passed in the street!

The bluebottles was quick, you had to admit it. They didn't waste no time.

"Come along with us, now, sensible and quiet," says Meatface, and gives a heave to the arm he'd got hold of. "Least said, soonest mended!"

"But my chicks! Let me make some arrangements! Let me go and tell my friends!"

"Oho!" says Toadstool, giving a heave to the other arm. "That's an old trick! I'm surprised at a clever old stick like yourself trying it on! Now, now, miss!" he shouted out in a fright, and lifted up his boot Jubilee-high. "Don't you try nothing with that there chopper!"

"Nor you neither, my lad!" warned Meatface, bunching a fist as big as a Bible, as Young Nick took the chopper off Jubilee, her being six inches too short to do any good with it. "It's only in storybooks that Jack's a giant-killer. In real life, it's the other way round! So let's have it quiet and easy. It'll be best for all concerned."

"But my friends, my friends!" wailed old Parrot Face, as the bluebottles dragged him downstairs. "Let me tell my friends!"

But there weren't no need. Smudgeon had already done it. He'd gone off like a puff of smoke as soon as the bluebottles had showed theirselves. So all Onion Court knew, and was ready and waiting, outside and in the hall.

"It wasn't my fault! It wasn't my fault!" Smudgeon kept crying, just like the cabdriver what had knocked down Whirling Willy in the fog. Only this time there weren't no doctor to come and help old Parrot Face, what had been knocked down worse. "I never knew they were following me! It wasn't my fault!"

But he shouldn't never have said nothing; then Jubilee wouldn't have gone for him like she done, mad as a cat, and his dad had to pull her off before Smudgeon's eyes was all red tears. And Meatface kept on saying, "Quiet and easy. Let's have it quiet and easy, now! It's best for everybody in the long run!"

Then the bluebottles took old Parrot Face off into the dark, with Jubilee trying to pull him back, and the Smudgeons following after, shouting out, not to worry, they'd do what they could for his chicks.

"MR. D.! MR. D.!" whispered Young Nick to the blanket what was hanging up across the corner of the Smudgeons' room—for what were the sense in running after the bluebottles and shouting himself hoarse?

Old Parrot Face was gone, and he wouldn't be coming back no more. Like the gent in the park had said, him with the chimney-pot hat: they was going to put old Parrot Face behind bars for the rest of his life.

"Mr. D.! Mr. D.!" Leastways, there was always the big feller, if Mr. D. was back from Liverpool at last, with his name. "Mr. D.! Mr. D.!"

"Give him a bit of peace!" came Mr. O'Grady's voice, and then his bristly head. "He's just come back from Liverpool, and he's sleeping like a babe!" Been traveling all night, y'know!"

"But I've got to talk to him about the big feller! I've got to!"

"Ah! That big feller!" says Mr. O'Grady, scratching his head. "From Kilkenny, wasn't he? Tell you what! I'll tie another knot in the tail of me shirt to remind me to ask Mr. D. as soon as he wakes up! Can't do fairer than that!"

"You can, you can!" shouts Young Nick—and before Mr. O'Grady can stop him, he's round the wrong side of the blanket and inside Mr. O'Grady's and Mr. D.'s private property!

"Mr. D.! Mr. D.!"

But all there was behind the blanket were Mr. O'Grady's bed, Mr. O'Grady's box of stinking clothes, Mr. O'Grady's big, black cooking-pot, and Mr. O'Grady his angry, bristly self!

"Where is he? Where's Mr. D.? You said he was asleep!"

"Just nipped up the chimney," says Mr. O'Grady, jerking his thumb. "Heard you coming, and up he went. Very private person, is Mr. D.!"

"You're a liar, you're a liar, and you'll burn in hellfire!" screamed Young Nick, fetching Mr. O'Grady a punch in the chest what set him back so's he sat down on his pot like he was ready for boiling. "There ain't no Mr. D. and there never was!"

"Of course there's a Mr. D.! Don't I talk to him every night about the old country, and the good things that are on the way tomorrow?"

"Liar, liar!"

"And didn't he say that he knew your big feller from Kilkenny?" went on Mr. O'Grady, nodding his head. "How could he have done such a thing if he wasn't a person at all? And don't all the Acre belong to him, which likewise he couldn't own unless he was a person? So use your common sense, me boy, and don't go punching a gentleman in the chest before his supper's gone down, and calling him a liar!"

There weren't no sense in talking no more. There weren't no sense in nothing no more.

"Look, me boy, look!" cried Mr. O'Grady, struggling up out of his pot. "I'm tying that knot in the tail of me shirt! Just as soon as Mr. D. comes down from the chimney, I'll ask him about Kilkenny! Big as a church, you said!"

But Young Nick, like Mr. D. himself, weren't there. He were over by the door.

"You're a naughty fellow," came Mr. O'Grady's voice from behind the blanket. "You're a naughty, naughty fellow, Mr. D.! Fancy building up that poor boy's hopes for nothing, and him from the old country too! You've broken his heart, Mr. D. Wicked, I call it!"

Chapter Fifteen

It were a cold night. Even old Parrot Face's blankets piled up on top didn't make much difference. It were a cold what come from inside, mostly.

"He done it because of that old fiddle," whispered Young Nick to Jubilee.

"It wasn't my fault!" mumbled Jubilee, just like all them others had done.

"Old Parrot Face."

"Our dad."

Then all the moaning and sobbing and sighing that went on in Onion Court of a nighttime, come up all round them, thick and gasping as fog.

"Let's go and have a look in the park," said Young Nick, when morning come at last—and gray as dust, it were—"before any folks wake up."

"What for?" asked Jubilee.

"Maybe he got away from them bluebottles and he's hiding up a tree again."

The park was quiet, and the grass were all sheeted over with mist, like it was undertaker dead.

"Dark the path that we are treading . . ." sang Jubilee, in her squeaky little voice, under every black and skinny tree.

But there weren't no bulky article hiding up among the branches, and there weren't no tin whistle what answered Jubilee's song.

"All through the night . . ."

They crept round the lake, to see if he'd fallen in; then they went to the wild side, to have a look in their old ivy and hawthorn home.

"It's him!" cried Jubilee. "He's inside!"

But it weren't old Parrot Face. It were a frowsy old gent wrapped up in rags and newspapers, what opened an eye like a stone.

"Shove off!" he said. "This here hole's mine!"

Then he saw Jubilee's gold earrings, and his other stone opened up, and it were shining, like there was a slug on it.

"Come over here, little girl," he said. "Let's have a better look at you!" and he reached out a hand what was clawed with broken nails, and Young Nick and Jubilee run for their lives, out of the park and back to Onion Court.

THERE WEREN'T GOING TO BE NO SCHOOL. They was to go to the police court with the Smudgeons, instead.

"Just so Mr. Owen can see that you're being properly looked after, dears," said Mrs. Smudgeon as they walked along. "It'll make him feel better before—before he goes away."

"And no shouting nor screaming," said Mr. Smudgeon, turning up his coat collar as it come on to rain. "It won't do no good." And Mrs. Smudgeon give a pat at her hair and says, "You just keep quiet and easy, dears, like the police gentleman said."

Then they come to the police court, which were up Piccadilly way, not far from where Whirling Willy got knocked down. And there was Meatface and Toadstool, waiting in the passage outside the courtroom, quiet and easy, along with a crowd of folk what looked frightened to death.

"I hope you've left your chopper at home," said Toadstool to Jubilee, looking her up and down. "Just take things quiet and easy, miss."

"And no more giants, Jack," says Meatface to Young Nick, looking *him* up and down. "Real life ain't like a beanstalk, lad! Climb up out of your proper station, and you'll just get knocked down again! So, like my friend here says, it's quiet and easy, lad, and you won't come to no harm."

Then they went into the courtroom and sat down at the back. It were a big, square, ugly room, with ugly walls and bluebottles standing by the door, and there were an ugly old magistrate sitting up on high, as proud as Old Nick. He were the ugliest gent Young Nick and Jubilee had ever seen. There weren't nothing what wouldn't be sniffed out by his long sharp nose, and there weren't nothing to be hoped for in his freezing hard eyes.

"Look!" cried out Jubilee, jumping up and pointing.

"Quiet!" whispered Mr. Smudgeon, pulling her down.

"But it's old Chimney Pot!"

"And easy, dear," whispers Mrs. Smudgeon, "like the police gentleman said."

But Jubilee were right. It were him! It were old Parrot Face's worst enemy, the gent what he'd robbed of the gold watch in the park! He were sitting right in front, just waiting to finish old Parrot Face off.

"Christmas Owen!" somebody called out very loud, and he give a little jump. Then in come old Parrot Face with a bluebottle behind him to stop him running off. But there weren't no need. He were all gray and shrunken, and more like a dead bird than ever, and he looked like he couldn't hardly walk.

"Our dad!" sobbed Jubilee as old Parrot Face was pushed up some steps and into a box with spikes in front so everybody could see him.

"Quiet!" whispered Mr. Smudgeon, but old Parrot Face had heard. And it did him a wonder of good—you had to admit it!—when he looked and see'd Young Nick and Jubilee sitting at the back! He straightened himself up and give one of his winks; then all of a sudden there come a terrible shout from the front!

"That's him! That's him all right!"

It were Chimney Pot! He'd jumped up from his seat, all red with the excitement of seeing old Parrot Face behind bars for the rest of his life! He couldn't hardly wait for the end!

"I'll never forget that ugly face," he shouts, "for as long as I live!"

"Sit down, sir!" says the magistrate, banging on his desk with a hammer. "Sit down and keep quiet! Have you no respect for this court? You will give your evidence at the proper time, sir, and you will give it on oath!"

So Chimney Pot had to sit down and bide his time and wait his turn, while Meatface and Toadstool got up, one after another, and told what had happened from beginning to end.

They told how Chimney Pot had laid a complaint that he'd been robbed of his watch, and it were robbery with violence as his weskit had been torn, and that made it a hundred times worse.

Then they told about the fifty-pound reward, and how the boy Smudgeon had come with the watch and taken the money back to Christmas Owen in Onion Court.

"And it was there that we apprehended him," said Meatface, "with his ill-gotten gains in his hand."

"And what did he say when you charged him?" asked the magistrate.

"He said that the watch hadn't been stolen, your honor, but found," said Meatface, and everybody laughed.

"Is this the watch?" asked the magistrate, holding it up, and it were the first time Young Nick and Jubilee had ever seen it with their eyes, though it had always been in Young Nick's thoughts. It didn't look much, swinging and shining on its chain—leastways, not compared with taking old Parrot Face away forever.

"That is the article, your honor," said Meatface, and stood down.

"And now, sir," said the magistrate to Chimney Pot, "you may give your evidence to the court."

"That's him, that's him!" cries Chimney Pot, jumping up again.

"You will give your evidence in the proper manner," says the magistrate, banging with his hammer again. "You will go to the witness stand and take the oath, sir. Only then will you be heard by this court."

"Come on!" whispers Young Nick to Jubilee, as Chimney Pot goes where he's been told and starts promising to tell the truth, the whole truth, and nothing but the truth so help him God, and old Parrot Face looks like all he's hoping for is a dirty lie. "Let's go and get some milk!"

"Now?"

"Now!" says Young Nick. "Ready—steady—GO!" And he gives her a great pinch and a shove!

"Leastways, you're still good at it!" mutters Young Nick, hopping over the benches quick as a flea, while Jubilee goes down with a scream and a shriek and starts jumping and jerking among all the frightened feet. "Even though it mayn't get you wed!"

Then he's up next to old Parrot Face, pulling away at his arm, while everybody's still gawping at Jubilee going through her antics, and shouting, "Give her air! Give her air!"

"Come on! Come on!" cries Young Nick, but old

Parrot Face were harder to move than a tree. The big feller would have known what to do! The big feller would have been up and away, with Jubilee under one arm and Young Nick under the other, and never stopping till they got to Kilkenny!

But not old Parrot Face. He just stood there, shaking his head and saying, "It's no good, it's no good, chick! We can't keep running forever!" And his eyes was full of tears.

Then it were all over.

"That's an old trick!" says Toadstool, getting hold of Young Nick by the collar.

"It's only in storybooks that folk get rescued at the last minute," says Meatface, getting hold of Young Nick by the hair. "In real life, they go to prison for years! So take it quiet and easy, lad," he says, dragging Young Nick away and holding on to him tight while two more bluebottles did likewise with Jubilee, who was all wild and staring, like a fox in the night. "Quiet and easy . . . it'll be best for all concerned."

Then the magistrate stopped banging with his hammer, and everybody quietened down, and the magistrate said he'd a good mind to send them two little animals to prison for contempt of court. But first of all he was going to deal with their father, who, judging by the behavior of his children, must be a very bad lot.

"And now, sir," he says to Chimney Pot, "you may give your evidence on oath. Is this the same man who robbed you of your watch?" And he points straight at old Parrot Face, who has to hold on to the spikes in front of him to keep himself from falling down.

Chimney Pot takes a good look. Then he looks at Young Nick and at Jubilee. Then he looks back at old Parrot Face and takes a deep breath.

"No, your honor," he says, and old Parrot Face falls down and a gent has to help him up again. "This is not the same man!"

"What?" shouts the magistrate, like he hadn't heard right.

"This is not the same man who robbed me," says Chimney Pot. "I thought I spoke plainly enough." And old Parrot Face stares like *he* hadn't heard right.

"But you just said—" cries the magistrate, beginning to go red.

"What I said, your honor, was not on oath. And as you yourself pointed out, the court can take no account of it. So I say again, and on oath, that this is not the same man who robbed me. He—he's as different as chalk from cheese."

"You—you are making a mockery of this court, sir! Don't you understand? You are asking me to set a thief free! Have you no respect for the laws of the land?"

"Not so much as I have for myself, your honor. After all, the laws are only made by men—but I have been made by God! *This is not the same man!*"

"You—you are a scoundrel, sir!" shouted the magistrate in a terrible rage. "Case dismissed!" And you never saw a gent so angry over having to do a good deed!

THEY WAS ALL IN THE PASSAGE outside the courtroom—
the Smudgeons, old Parrot Face, and his chicks—and
they was all laughing and crying at the same time, and
shaking old Parrot Face by the hand and thumping
him on the back like he'd done something wonderful!

"Mr. Owen, Mr. Owen!"

It were Chimney Pot, wanting a last word with
the different man.

"You asked me for the time once, I remember," he
says, taking out his gold watch—for he'd knowed all
along it was the same man. Once you'd see'd old Parrot Face, you couldn't never forget him! "Well," he
says, looking more at old Parrot Face than his watch,
"it's nearly twelve o'clock."

Old Parrot Face blinked and stared.

"Why, sir," he asked, very quiet, "why did you
change your mind?"

"Let's say, rather," said Chimney Pot, putting
away his watch, "that it was a change of heart. And
the heart, my friend," he said, with a look at Young
Nick and Jubilee, "sometimes has better eyes than
the mind!"

"The money, sir! The fifty pound! I'll give it
back!"

"Keep it," said Chimney Pot as he walked away.
"I fancy you will put it to a better use than ever I
could, my friend!"

Chapter Sixteen

So JUBILEE GOT HER OLD FIDDLE AFTER ALL, and the gent in the violin shop said he'd knowed all along it would happen, and it would have been a crime if the little musical lady hadn't got it. And old Parrot Face winked because *he* knowed it were on account of a crime that she had!

"And now, chicks," says old Parrot Face when they got home and Jubilee was stroking her fiddle like it was the cat, "it'll be up Piccadilly way and round Leicester Square for us three Owens together!"

"But what'll happen when Mr. Willy starts rendering again?" asked Young Nick. "He don't like us much."

But it were all right. They found out that Whirling Willy was thinking of joining up with the cabdriver what had knocked him down and brung him a bunch of grapes, and what turned out to be fond of playing the bassoon of an evening.

"And your bassoon," said Whirling Willy, scratching away at his white treetrunk of a leg, "is your very good earner indeed!"

But it weren't no better than your vox humana and your old violin! Them three Owens did wonderful well up Piccadilly way and round Leicester Square of an evening after school.

Sometimes, Young Nick, what was quick at figures and never let one get away without paying out for his treat, come back with as much as twelve shilling in the hat!

"Fancy that, now!" said old Parrot Face when he were told, for he never counted up nothing for himself, as him and Jubilee wasn't so clever at sums as was Young Nick. "It looks like we've got our feet on the ladder, chicks, and we're on our way up!" And when it come round to Christmastime, and they started rendering "Good King Wenceslas" and "Hark the Herald," he couldn't hardly believe it when Young Nick come back with more than a pound sometimes!

"It just shows you, chicks," he sighed. "It just shows you!" But he never said what.

Then it were Christmas Eve and old Parrot Face kept his promise to Mr. Rummer and come along to St. John's Church to sing with the boys in the choir, and it were a real shame you couldn't take the hat round, as old Parrot Face never done better, and there was hundreds of folk listening, and there'd have been ten pound if there'd been a penny!

You should have seen him standing there with all them Blewcoat boys and their forest of daffodil legs, and singing like he never sung before! He done "God Rest Ye" best, and when he come to "tidings of comfort and joy," his voice swelled out like a great bell, and it filled up the church, right to the roof. And it were a big church, too!

Afterwards, Mr. Rummer come back with them all to Onion Court, to take a glass of something warming, what Mrs. Smudgeon had got ready, if the cat hadn't got there first.

They walked from the church together, still in their yellow and blue: Young Nick and Smudgeon with Jubilee in the middle, tossing her bonnet from side to side. But it didn't matter no more. Jubilee, with her gold earrings and old violin, had got dowry enough to wed where she chose, even if it did turn out to be Smudgeon, and him only prospects and skin and bone!

"My compliments, Mr. Owen," says Mrs. Smudgeon when they all come in, and she sees Mr. Rummer what she wasn't expecting, "but I'd be obliged if you'd favor me with a lend back of them two glasses what you borrowed last June."

Then, when old Parrot Face had gone upstairs, she unwraps Parliament like she was peeling an onion what was crying of itself.

"This is our youngest, Mr. Rummer," she says. "I hope that you'll soon be having little Parliament here to be studying at the Blewcoat School." And she gives a ladylike pat at her hair.

"It will be a pleasure, ma'am!" says Mr. Rummer, with an admiring blink. "I look forward very much to teaching Parliament reading, writing, and especially Bible!"

Then in comes old Parrot Face, and Parliament gets wrapped up and put away, and Mrs. Smudgeon fills up all the glasses.

"A merry Christmas!" cries Mr. Smudgeon, lifting his glass and giving a terrible longing look at Mr. Rummer's walking stick what was standing up in a corner, and what would have chopped up a treat.

Then it were merry Christmases all round, and down went Mrs. Smudgeon's warming, which were English courage and not so strong as Dutch.

"And now let's drink to another merry Christmas!" cries Mr. Rummer, holding out his glass for another fill, and not looking like a schoolmaster anymore, on account of not being used to anything stronger than milk. "Let's drink to Mr. Christmas Owen! All our thanks to you, sir, for your singing! In all my life, I never heard so large and fine a voice coming from—if you'll pardon the expression, sir—so small a man!"

"But he ain't small!" shouts out Young Nick of a sudden. "Didn't you hear him? Our dad's a big feller, big as a church!" And everybody laughed, but nobody called him a liar.

Author's Note

The Blewcoat School was one of several charity schools in the City of Westminster. Founded by philanthropists in the eighteenth century, and supported by public subscription, they gave a good education to the children of the poor and helped to settle them in respectable trades. Each school was distinguished by the color of its uniform. There was a Browncoat School, a Greencoat School, a Greycoat School (still in use) and, of course, the Blewcoat School, which was built in 1709 by William Green, a prosperous brewer, whose heart was in the right place but whose spelling, alas, was not.

About the Author

Leon Garfield is the author of many highly acclaimed books for young readers. His novel *Devil-in-the-Fog* won the Manchester Guardian Award for Children's Fiction, and *Smith* was awarded the Arts Council Prize, the Prix de la Fondation de France, and the Children's Literature Association's Phoenix Award. Other books by Leon Garfield include *Footsteps, The Night of the Comet,* and *The Strange Affair of Adelaide Harris.*

Mr. Garfield is married to the writer Vivien Alcock and lives in London.